Kidnap in Dalham

United States Deputy Marshal Ned Thomas is awaiting the arrival of two men who plan to kill him, when he receives an assignment from the US Army. He is to report to General Stanmore in Dalham. But why has he been chosen, despite the mutual hatred which exists between them? He is tempted to disobey orders, but his sense of duty prevails and he travels to Dalham.

Within a single day he goes from hero to suspected killer and is initially sentenced to hang. But his sentence is commuted to life imprisonment at the notorious Yukron Valley State Penitentiary, where many would have preferred a quiet death.

Now he must face danger from every quarter. Can he distinguish friend from foe and can he clear his name? Only time will tell.

Kidnap in Dalham

BILL WILLIAMS

A Black Horse Western

ROBERT HALE · LONDON

ISBN 0 7090 7668 1

Robert Hale Limited
Clerkenwell House
Clerkenwell Green
London EC1R 0HT

Typeset by
Derek Doyle & Associates, Liverpool.
Printed and bound in Great Britain by
Antony Rowe Limited, Wiltshire

ONE

United States Deputy Marshal Ned Thomas had been preparing for the arrival of two men who had escaped from prison and, according to his informant, the Carter brothers planned to kill him. Now, he had to leave and hope that he would be back in time to stop the men taking their revenge on the town. When the US Army courier had arrived with details of a special assignment, he had sent a wire message to his marshal, John Patterson, to enlist his help in arranging for someone else to take his place. The reply was short and clear, it read: 'Outside my authority. Imperative you travel to Dalham as ordered.'

Unless Thomas intended to disobey an order for the first time in his life he would be on the train tomorrow and on his way to report to General Charles S. Stanmore in Dalham City. If he missed tomorrow's train out of Statton Crossing he would be stranded there for another week.

Ned Thomas was fifty-three years old and a good three inches taller than most men. There was a good crop of steely grey hair beneath the dark leather Stetson that only ever left his head at bedtime. In certain light, his dark-brown eye appeared almost as black as the patch that covered the gruesome disfigurement. Smiling didn't come easy to Thomas. Maybe it was because his life experiences had given him very little reason to do so. There were just the faintest beginnings of a paunch, but he still presented an awesome-looking figure with his wide shoulders and thick neck. He was in better condition than many younger men, but he was beginning to think that he'd lost the edge that he needed. Maybe a crafty gunslinger would get on his blind side to gain an advantage. He'd ridden his luck for nearly five years since he'd lost the eye when a broken bottle had been thrust in it during a bar room brawl when he'd gone to the aid of a sheriff who was outnumbered. It hadn't stopped him killing the man who had thrown away the bottle and gone for his gun.

Thomas and General Stanmore had met during the war and the general was not on his list of favourite people. In fact, he hated the man and was certain that the feeling was mutual. Thomas had groaned when Stanmore took up his present post last year, even though he thought it was unlikely that their paths would cross, despite knowing that the general could make use of any US marshal or their deputies for special operations. It was baffling to him as to why the general would call on his services, unless he was absolutely desperate or the assignment was likely to cause Thomas some grief.

*

The sun was just coming up by the time he double checked the straps that secured the extras that he would be taking on the long journey. He would be unpacking in less than an hour when he caught the weekly train out of Statton Crossing, the town which he used as a base.

Statton Crossing was situated almost in the middle of the territory that fell within his jurisdiction even though most of the population was to the north. He had warned the town sheriff, Len Luckings about the threat from the Carter brothers and told him that Marshal Patterson would be sending some help, but it wouldn't arrive until after Thomas had left. He couldn't tell Luckings too much about his assignment, because the message from the general's office had contained a special code indicating that his assignment would be top secret. He didn't like cloak-and-dagger assignments, but he accepted that they were necessary on special occasions.

'I'm surprised you're leaving town, Marshal. I heard you were expecting some trouble,' said Chatty Broom, after Thomas had ordered his ticket to Dalham.

'There mightn't be any trouble, and if there is Sheriff Luckings will take care of things. So don't you go frightening people with one of your rumours, otherwise I'll be having words with you when I get back.' Broom was the town gossip, but he would be keeping his mouth shut after the warning from Thomas.

Once he unloaded his supplies, he led the black stallion up the ramp into the cattle wagon and settled it in. He had paid more for the thorough-bred than it would have cost for six animals from normal breeding stock, and it was his pride and joy. He intended checking on him during the stops the train would make before it reached Dalham, the second largest city in the state.

Three years ago, Thomas had been on the verge of taking up the post of sheriff in his home town of Hinklyville when John Patterson had asked him to become a deputy marshal. Thomas had known John Patterson a long time and he respected him, because unlike some, he paid his deputies a decent wage and he wasn't corrupt. Thomas also admired Patterson for the way that he'd adapted to the administration work that was the main part of a marshal's duties. The real work was done by the deputies and Thomas had been involved in solving all manner of crimes, including organized rustling and illegal arms trading, but most of the time he was helping to break up notorious gangs, or hunting down a wanted man. It had been the ideal job for Thomas with his wide experience, but his next assignment would be the first one working for the military.

TWO

General Charles S. Stanmore had been on the point of retiring the previous year after a distinguished career in the army when he was persuaded to take charge of the special law enforcement agency which he had helped create. Now he was thinking that he had made a big mistake. If the current special operations case went wrong they would want a high-ranking scapegoat, and he would be it.

Stanmore poured himself another large brandy and then continued pacing up and down his office at the government building in Dalham. He would have appeared a contradiction to those who believed that you could tell a man's background from his face. The busted, bulbous nose and heavily scarred face was permanently reddened by high blood pressure and the side effects of the large amounts of wine and brandy that he consumed despite medical advice that he was shortening his life. He scoffed at the suggestion of prolonging it: what life did he have now that his active service was over? Stanmore was from one of the wealthiest families in the state. He had benefited from all the trappings of wealth, including a good education with the chance of a life of luxury which he had spurned in favour of a career in the military.

He heeded his father's advice that having a wife was beneficial to a politician, but a hindrance to a professional soldier. By the time he had achieved his ambition he had become set in his ways and marriage was no longer an option. He had been content with a string of whores and although he no longer sought sexual pleasure, he still arranged for women to spend the night in his bed. They got to have an uninterrupted night's sleep and he kept up the pretence of the big virile soldier.

He was fifty-six years old which was not the age of a warrior, for that is what he had considered himself, not in the physical sense, but spiritually. Dying in a rocking chair at some home for retired officers wasn't the way he hoped to end his days. At least the man he was about to condemn to an early grave would have the privilege of dying with dignity and in action. He would be on active service for his country. He would die with honour even if he couldn't be given any choice in the matter. Stanmore wasn't trying to convince himself of the rights and wrongs of condemning a man to death. He had sent hundreds of soldiers to a needless death because of his mistakes in battle, and it had never bothered him. He wouldn't be losing any sleep over the fate of a tin-pot deputy marshal like Ned Thomas.

Stanmore and Thomas went back a long way and

had first met during the early part of the war when Stanmore was a major. By the time the war ended, Stanmore was a full general and Thomas was a sergeant. He had once overheard a group of men talking about Thomas and one had remarked that Thomas was too brave and intelligent to be an officer. Those comments had always rankled with Stanmore. Well the ex-sergeant would get his chance to be brave.

The knock on the door caused Stanmore to stop pacing and growl, 'Enter.'

The soldier stood stiffly to attention. 'Telegram for the general, sir.'

He waited until the soldier had retreated from his office before he sat down, gulped some brandy and then unfolded the telegram which told him that Deputy Marshal Ned Thomas had boarded the train out of Statton Crossing bound for Dalham.

Stanmore banged the top of his desk with a clenched first. 'Good man, or should I say, you stupid peasant.'

The following day Stanmore's mood would be changed by the receipt of another telegram telling him that Thomas's train had not arrived at Googan's Bluff. It was six hours late and there was no news of what might have happened to it.

THREE

When the train stopped at Saratone Station, Thomas was looking forward to stretching his legs. The seats on the train were not exactly comfortable, especially for someone with legs as long as his. The next part of the journey would be across a stretch of open desert and he planned to take in plenty of liquid refreshment during his short stay in town. The woman who had got on at Phelan's Post was attractive enough, at least from the distance of three seats away, but he'd wished that she hadn't spent so much time staring at him. Perhaps some women had a sixth sense about a widower man, not realizing that he wasn't as wealthy as he looked with him wearing his best travelling clothes, including a fancy purple and gold waistcoat. Whatever it was, she hadn't been deterred by his scowl and he'd opted for looking out of the window.

As Thomas limped his way towards the animal wagon, the limp being the result of a bullet in the hip, the woman was being embraced by some city dude who must have been worth a dollar or two.

Thomas's ma had always told him not to judge a man by his clothes, but he had found it to be a useful indicator. More often than not it meant that the wearer of fine clothes was a thief of some kind even though what he did might be legal. The woman broke away from the man, who was old enough to be her daddy, but the kiss and the way that she had pressed her body against him made that unlikely. She smiled once more at Thomas.

'Thank you for being such pleasant company, Marshal,' she said, causing her companion to frown and Thomas to shake his head and mutter 'Women'. He didn't know how she knew he was a marshal because he wasn't displaying any badge.

Once the stallion was saddled up, he led it across the street to the water trough near the Friendly Drinker saloon and then headed inside. He intended having a few beers first and then he would exercise the horse by taking it for a short ride. The barman was picking his nose and the heavily painted woman standing near the bar was scratching one of her armpits. The only other occupant was a greasy-looking fellow who hadn't seen a bath this side of Christmas, and it was now the month of July.

He ordered two beers and the barman had the decency to wipe his nose-picking hand on his shirt sleeve before he served him. Thomas hoped that in the short time he planned to stay in this seedy establishment he would be allowed to drink in peace, but it was not to be. The painted woman sidled up on his blind side, but the cheap perfume hit his nostrils before she drew alongside.

'Are you expecting company, handsome?' she asked, obviously alluding to the two drinks that had appeared in front of him. Thomas placed several coins on the bar before replying, 'Only my own,' and then he downed the first drink, not expecting his rebuff to have the desired effect, and he wasn't wrong.

'Why don't you bring that other drink upstairs to my room?' she suggested. 'It's much cooler than down here and I can promise that you won't be disappointed with what's on offer. It won't cost you much more that you just paid for those drinks, and it'll help you relax. Marlon here can vouch for that.'

The irritation left him, and he smiled at the thought that smelly Marlon was being revealed as a former customer. Thomas's mood was lightened by the conversation and he decided to go easy on the pathetic woman. He turned towards her, looked her up and down as though he was assessing the goods, and then told her that he would finish his beer before deciding what to do.

Painted lady smiled and Marlon grinned because he usually got to watch from the spy hole in the wall that joined the room where the 'entertainment' took place.

Marlon was thinking that the old feller was a bit long in the tooth so it should last longer than usual. Vicky would be able to file and paint all her nails while old one eye was panting and grunting. If Vicky was feeling generous he might get a free one if the old guy hadn't managed to satisfy her.

Dopey Marlon knew that Vicky didn't ply her

14

trade just for the money because she'd told him that she liked men and that's why she'd never married despite lots of proposals when she was younger and prettier. Vicky decided a long time ago that one man was never going to be enough for her. So, she had solved her problem and earned a living at the same time.

Marlon wouldn't try robbing this one. He might be old, but there was something real mean about him. That staring eye had already given Marlon the creeps, but still it fascinated him.

Thomas sighed, placed two coins on the bar and then declared that one was for the lady. The other one was for Marlon to pay for a bath, and if he had any change then he was to give it to the barman to buy a handkerchief in the hope that he might keep his finger out of his nose. His remarks had clearly taken the painted lady by surprise, but didn't appear to have registered with smelly Marlon who was still studying Thomas and asked, 'Why are you wearing that patch, mister? Is there something wrong with your eye?'

It wasn't the first time that Thomas had been asked such a dumb question and he decided to give Marlon one of his stock responses. It involved Thomas moving really close to Marlon's pimpled face, and then lifting the patch to reveal the gruesome hole which had once held his missing eye.

'Perhaps you would like to remove the speck of dust I got in it,' Thomas suggested. Marion wasn't the brightest of individuals or the most sensitive but the empty eye socket had him on the verge of puking. Thomas replaced the patch and walked out, leaving the odd threesome speechless.

He was looking forward to his short ride to the outskirts of town but the smartly dressed man standing by his horse had other ideas. When Thomas reached for the reins that were tied to the hitch rail, the man smiled as he addressed him. 'It's your lucky day, mister.'

Thomas glared at the man to whom he had taken an instant dislike.

'And why would that be? If you plan on trying to sell me something, then forget it. Now I suggest you move out of the way unless you want to risk getting a hoof in your balls.'

The smile left the dude's face, and he appeared anxious as he glanced over to the man who was sitting in the carriage across Main Street.

'I'm sorry, sir. We seem to have got off on the wrong foot,' said the dude, hoping to recover the situation. 'I'm here to offer you one thousand dollars for your horse. Mr Kennet over there is a very wealthy man, and he wants me to purchase this fine specimen on his behalf.'

Thomas glanced over at the fat man who was seated in the carriage and puffing on the largest cigar that he had ever seen. The offer was tempting, especially with his retirement not too far off. Then he would only require an animal that could ferry him back and forth on his fishing trips, and although his needs were simple, the $1,000 would come in handy.

'Of course you can keep your saddle and take your pick from the horses in the corral at the back of Markham's Smithy at the end of Main Street. Mr Kennet will pay for a more modest animal to replace this one.'

Thomas repositioned his eye patch, something that he often did when deliberating. He didn't like making spot decisions, but this was too good to turn down.

'I'm tempted, but I would want the money now because I need to get somewhere in a hurry. I can't wait for a bank to open or someone to ride off and fetch it.'

'I have it right here,' said Tyler, as he tapped his pocket. 'Mr Kennet is always ready to do business, that's why he's a wealthy man. By the way, my name's Henry Tyler.' Thomas shook the outstretched hand, but he didn't volunteer his own name.

He watched Tyler carefully as he reached inside his smart city suit and produced the envelope that was bulging with dollar bills. The smile on Tyler's face widened when Thomas nodded in agreement when he was asked if they had a deal.

'I think you've just done a piece of smart business and Mr Kennet's judgement has let him down on this occasion. If you unpack your belongings I'll hand over the money and then take the horse over to Mr Kennet. You can go and choose your replacement mount, and I'll join you there so I can settle up with Markham. Would you like to keep your old saddle or choose a new one?'

'I'll be keeping it,' Thomas replied.

'Then I'll bring it up to Markham's for you,' Tyler offered.

Thomas removed his things from the stallion and placed them on the steps of the saloon. He patted the horse and felt a Judas when he took the bulging envelope from Tyler.

'Right, I'll see you in a few minutes,' Tyler said, and then suggested, 'Perhaps we can have a drink together before you head off? You might want to count that bundle before you go.'

Thomas unbuttoned his shirt and stuffed the envelope inside it. He didn't intend having a drink with Tyler or face the odd occupants of the saloon again.

When Thomas arrived at Markham's livery it was deserted, so he sauntered around the back and leaned on the corral fence, while he studied the five horses. The grey sorrel caught his eye, and provided a closer inspection didn't reveal an injury it would be his new mount.

When he made his way back to the rundown livery he was getting anxious about the train's departure. He was relieved when he saw a man tying on a blacksmith's apron and after he determined that he was Jack Markham he explained why he was there.

'I'd like to buy the grey sorrel out at the back. Henry Tyler should be here soon and he'll settle up for Kennet who has just bought my horse.'

Jack Markham gave Thomas a puzzled look. 'Sorry, mister, but none of the horses out back are for sale. They belong to the army who will be picking

18

them up once I've fitted them with new shoes and branded them. In any case, I've never heard of the two names that you mentioned. I can tell you that they're not from these parts, unless they've never owned a horse, because I know everyone who does.'

Thomas was the one looking puzzled now. 'Tyler's a tall, skinny dude with a thin moustache and Kennet's a fat guy who was puffing on a king-size cigar when I saw him about twenty minutes ago sitting in a fancy-looking open carriage.'

Markham could see that the one-eyed stranger was anxious but he couldn't see how he could help him, except tell him that he probably knew one of the men he'd just described, but his name wasn't Kennet.

'The fat guy, as you calls him, sounds like Melvin Pettifer, our undertaker, but I've no idea who the other feller might be.'

Thomas didn't know what was happening, but at least he had the money and that was the main thing. If he had to pay for a replacement horse and saddle he would still be making a handsome profit on the sale of the stallion. When he pulled out the envelope from inside his shirt and thumbed through the wad of paper, the air was blue with cursing and his face reddened with anger. The envelope contained more blank paper than dollar bills. He didn't bother to determine how much money was in the bundle before he threw it to the ground and hurried away in the direction of the saloon, leaving Markham bemused and wondering what the hell was happening.

Thomas's bedroll, water canteen and other bits and pieces were still in the same spot. The saddle had gone, but at least the fat man and his carriage hadn't moved from across the street, and that's where Thomas headed.

'Are you Kennet?' Thomas growled, but wasn't sure why he'd bothered.

'Melvin Pettifer's my name, stranger, quality undertaker of this fine town. I once buried a Luke Kennet who was passing through when he got himself shot over a woman in the saloon over there. I can tell you that there ain't anyone who goes by the name of Kennet in town. Why do you ask?'

Thomas ignored his question and asked if he had seen Tyler.

'You mean the feller who you sold that fine horse to? Now, he was a strange one. He gets off the train, strolls around town chatting to anyone who comes by, purchases your horse and then gets back on the train.'

Thomas's spirits lifted and he turned his head in the direction of the station. He was soon cursing again when Pettifer told him that the train had left five minutes ago. Thomas pulled out the big gold-plated watch from the pocket of his fancy waistcoat.

'But the train wasn't due to leave for another ten minutes.'

Pettier shrugged his flabby shoulders. 'It some-times leaves earlier than planned if everyone is back on board. I've known folk travel thirty miles or more and miss the train because it left before it should. Perhaps they thought you were back on board when they saw your horse was loaded on.'

Thomas was thinking that it was more likely that the trickster Tyler had told the guard a pack of lies. Whatever the reason, Thomas wanted the stallion back and he had just thought of a way to do it.

'Where's the telegraph office, mister?'

The undertaker told him that despite having the railroad, the town didn't have a telegraph office or a sheriff. This time there was no cursing from Thomas, he just turned and headed back towards Markham's. The next train wouldn't be due for a week and he was certain that whatever plans General Stanmore had in store for him they wouldn't keep until then. Stanmore would have his hide and enjoy doing it.

Markham handed over the small amount of money that had been in the envelope and agreed to sell Thomas his own horse, a black gelding. It would be like riding a mule after the stallion, but at least he would be able to continue his journey. He planned to find a town where he could telegraph Stanmore to explain the reason for his delay. He also hoped that he could arrange to have Tyler arrested when the train stopped somewhere on the way to Dalham. Whatever happened he vowed to himself that he would track down Tyler one day, even if it was the last thing that he did.

By the time Thomas had loaded up the gelding and bought some supplies at the store, he figured that there was about three hours of daylight left but he intended riding through the night if he could see his way in the moonlight.

He had been riding for less than two hours when the black clouds appeared and the rain came, causing him to make camp for the night under the shelter of some trees. At least his luck hadn't deserted him completely because finding a tree in this area was as rare as the heavy rainfall. He prepared a meal of cold salted beef and beans after he'd given up trying to light a fire with the damp wood. Thomas wasn't the type to let the upset of being swindled affect either his appetite or his sleep and he curled up in his bedroll while he tucked into the food.

When Thomas's sleep was disturbed early the following morning, he wasn't sure if the cause was the neighing of his horse, the early morning sun, or the strange clanging noise. He remembered dozing off before he had finished his meal but the metal plate that lay beside him had been licked clean by someone or something. He turned towards the sound of the neighing horse and when he saw the gelding he was reminded of yesterday, and his meeting with Tyler. He rose to his feet, stretched the stiffness from his body and then walked towards the clump of trees and the direction of the clanging sound. He soon hurried back to where his belongings lay and frantically searched in one of the bags. Once he had pulled out the telescope he had won from an army scout during a game of cards, he ran back through the trees to the spot where he could view the railway track below. It was a long time since anything had made Ned Thomas tremble, but he did as he tried to focus the instrument. What he saw made him feel that the gods were smiling on him. Tethered to the side of the train was his stolen stallion. He shifted the scope towards the engine and saw three men. Two of them were railroad men and one of them was doing something to the giant connecting rod. The third man was Tyler.

Thomas hoisted the heavy saddle on to the gelding's back and then fumbled to tie the straps. As he pulled the last of the straps tight, he heard the sound of the train's hooter which he feared meant that the train was about to move off. He cursed when his foot missed the stirrup but he was soon mounted and heeling the gelding in the direction where he intended descending the small hill towards the track below. He didn't need his scope to see that the stallion wasn't there and that the three men had boarded the train. The gelding was doing well keeping its footing, but by the time they reached the flat ground the train was already in motion. Thomas directed his mount to follow the train which was moving very slowly, allowing him to soon draw level with the last carriage. He heeled the gelding hard, hoping for more speed and it responded at the same time as the train's speed increased. Thomas had been tempted to fire a few shots in the hope that the train might be stopped, but thought it more likely that the guard would return the fire.

As the train gathered more speed, he started to

lose ground and, as the last carriage passed him, Thomas saw Tyler. There was no trace of surprise on the trickster's face as he smiled down at him. Thomas could easily lip read Tyler's mocking words, 'Nice horse'. Thomas was about to pull up the gelding when its legs collapsed, and the horse crumpled beneath him, causing Thomas to hit the hard ground beside the track with a thud. He was shaken, but unhurt apart from a badly bruised shoulder, and angry when he saw that the gelding had not got off so lightly.

As the train drew away from them, Thomas knelt beside the distressed animal and stroked its neck while he eased his gun from the holster. The single shot ended the animal's suffering but it didn't ease Thomas's sadness. He had killed many men in the line of duty and had few regrets, but there was something different about killing an animal. Thomas's sadness turned to anger again as he looked along the track and saw that the train had stopped once more. He doubted that it was anything to do with him chasing after the train and more likely that it had suffered another mechanical problem. Thomas wasn't used to walking far, but he managed a brisk pace, driven by rage as he headed in the direction of the stranded train. When he was within twenty yards of the last carriage he saw three figures standing near the cattle wagon, one of whom was Tyler.

Tyler was desperate as he ordered the guards to release the stallion, but the guard was in no mood to be bossed by the fancy dude. Tyler was momentarily relieved when he saw Thomas stop and pull something from his pocket, and hoped that it might be some kind of medication. With luck, Thomas might be on the point of collapse from the exertion of the chase, but he was mistaken. Despite Tyler's hollering, by the time that the ramp had been lowered from the cattle wagon, Thomas was close enough for Tyler to see the rage on his face. He didn't carry a weapon and frantically sought the help of the armed guard by pointing owards Thomas and shouting, 'He's a madman. He'll kill me if you don't stop him. Shoot him! He thinks that I stole his horse, but I bought it fair and square. I swear on my dear ma's life I'm telling the truth.'

'I don't plan to shoot anyone for you, mister, especially a lawman,' replied the guard.

When Tyler spotted the marshal's badge pinned to Thomas's waistcoat, he turned and started running towards the front of the train, expecting Thomas to give chase. But Thomas had no intention of running after the younger man and fired two shots close enough to Tyler to cause him to pitch forward on to the ground. Tyler instinctively reached out to stop his fall, and the sound of his breaking wristbone was music to Thomas's ears. When Tyler stopped whimpering, he repeated over and over again, 'Don't kill me'.

He was still saying it when Thomas sauntered up and told him to get up. He had returned his weapon to its holster and he was hoping that Tyler would put up some sort of fight, even if he did only have the use of one hand. Fighting was the last thing on Tyler's mind as he cowered, rolling himself up like an unborn baby, in an attempt to protect himself.

'Where's that slick smile gone, you horse-thief?' said Thomas, before ordering Tyler to walk back to the cattle wagon where Thomas introduced himself to the guard, and told him that Tyler had stolen the stallion and was now under arrest.

The guard gave Tyler a dirty look and turned to Thomas. 'He told us that you had sold him the horse because you were going to shack up with Vicky in Saratone, that's why we didn't wait for you to get on board.'

'What!' gasped Thomas, perishing the thought. He moved towards the cowering Tyler who had braced himself for a beating, but Thomas reached into Tyler's pocket and pulled out his wallet. Thomas took enough money to cover the cost of the gelding and the saddle, and then threw the wallet at Tyler.

Thomas was pleased to be reunited with his stallion, but Tyler presented a problem. If the engine could be fixed again then he could hand Tyler over at the next town they stopped at that had a lawman. But that would involve paperwork, and having to tell how he was hoodwinked by Tyler would be embarrassing. So, Thomas decided to administer his own justice for once. It would save time and it was no more than the crook deserved.

Tyler was ordered to stay put while Thomas walked down the track and asked the railroad man covered in oil, if the engine could be fixed. He had never heard the accent that the reply was given in, or the name Jock, which is what the guard called the engine fixer. If Thomas had understood Jock correctly, then the train would be on the move again in about half an hour, so he hurried back to the cattle wagon and saddled up the stallion, and then told Tyler to mount up. Tyler was puzzled and stopped whimpering long enough to ask, 'Why, what are you going to do with me?'

'We're going for a short ride,' Thomas replied, and then roared at Tyler, 'Now get moving.'

Tyler winced with the pain from his wrist before finally managing to ease himself into the saddle, and then made another desperate plea to the guard.

'Don't let him take me. He'll kill me. Can't you see that he'll shoot me once we're away from any witnesses?'

The rail guard who had been the victim of horse-theft, spat on the ground. 'I could tell you were a slippery customer as soon as you got on the train. I hope the marshal finds a tree that's high enough to hang you from. You ain't worth wasting a bullet on. Stealing a man's horse is worse than stealing his wife.'

Thomas positioned himself behind Tyler and then heeled the animal to move off.

'Make sure you hold the train for me,' Thomas shouted back at the guard, as he guided the stallion away from the track and in the direction of the trees on the hill where he had camped.

It took him longer than expected to sort out the

problem of getting rid of Tyler and when he started to descend the hill for the second time the sound of train's hooter spooked the stallion, but he stayed sure-footed. When they reached the flat, he could see the guard urging him to hurry along.

'Did you hang that dude, Marshal?' the guard asked.

'What do you think?' Thomas asked, still wondering if the guard had a wife and if so, what she looked like after his earlier comments to Tyler about horse-stealing.

'To be honest, Marshal, I've had a bet with Oily Jock, the engineer. So I'm hoping you found a good strong tree up on that hill.'

'I was going to. I even selected the tree and uncoiled the rope, but it didn't seem right somehow. I did ask him if he wanted to be hanged, but he chose the other option.'

The guard was puzzled because he hadn't heard a shot, although he'd noticed that the marshal was carrying a large pearl-handled bowie knife. Perhaps he'd slit the horse-thief's throat. 'So how did you kill him, Marshal?'

'I didn't kill him, but it was tempting. I've never known a man squeal so much as that feller did. I offered to hang him or let him go. He chose to try and walk back to Saratone Station.'

The guard looked towards the burning sun. 'I think he made a bad choice, Marshal, but it means I've lost five dollars.'

Thomas looked back along the track in the direction of Saratone Station and remembered his journey across the desert yesterday and was inclined to agree with the guard.

The train had covered a good few miles before Thomas felt confident that it might make it all the way to Dalham.

FOUR

The train pulled into the station at Dalham almost a day late and Thomas was wondering what lay in store for him now. With luck, his assignment would have been allocated to someone else and he could head straight home and hope to be in time to tackle the Carter brothers. He didn't have long to wait to find out when the immaculately dressed officer approached him while he supervised the unloading of the stallion.

'Marshal Thomas?' he asked, and without waiting for an answer he introduced himself. 'Welcome to Dalham. I'm Major Linford from General Stanmore's department. Matters have become more urgent because of your late arrival due to the train problems. I'm to escort you to his office.'

Major Linford offered his hand to a disappointed Thomas who had just discovered he was still required for the assignment.

'I appreciate the urgency, Major, but I need to take care of my horse first, and then I'll follow you.'

'You needn't worry about your horse, but I would

understand if you were concerned about him. He's a fine-looking animal, but my men will make sure that he's stabled, and your belongings taken to your quarters.'

A military wagon pulled by two dark-grey horses was waiting for them outside the station, and the young soldier who had been leaning against the wagon sprang to attention when he spotted the major. Thomas hadn't visited Dalham in a long time and he was surprised how much it had changed. Now it was like he imagined a small eastern city would look like, with its tree-lined streets and fine buildings. He noted that the passers-by all looked kitted out in their Sunday best and he hadn't seen a single man who was carrying a weapon. Linford must have been reading his thoughts.

'I don't think you'll have much use for your pistol here, Marshal. I suggest that you leave it with me and I'll have it serviced in the armoury. It'll be ready for you when you go off on your assignment, that's if you need it. If you give it to me before you see the general, I'll make sure that it's done straight away.'

Thomas would feel naked without it, but the offer of a free service would be welcome and save him the job of cleaning it.

'Much obliged, Major. You mentioned my assignment and I'd appreciate some details. My orders were a bit vague, but it sounded very urgent. I'm puzzled why I was ordered to come all this way when there must be some local men who could have covered it. Is it military or civilian business?'

Major Linford looked serious when he replied,

'I'm sorry, Marshal, but the assignment is Code Five.'

'Code Five! What the hell is that supposed to mean?' growled Thomas.

Linford explained that Code Five was the highest security classification, which meant that he couldn't discuss the details with Thomas, even if he knew them.

Thomas had been hoping to have at least some idea of what was involved before meeting Stanmore. It was a meeting he wasn't looking forward to. When Thomas had left the army he had hoped that he would never hear the name Stanmore again, and never expected their paths to cross.

Thomas had been irritated more than once over the years when he had read in newspapers of Stanmore the hero, receiving yet another award. Thomas wondered if the folks in Washington knew what an incompetent, selfish, uncaring bully Stanmore was.

During the train journey he had mentally rehearsed how he would cope with meeting Stanmore and not react to him. Thomas prided himself on being a professional and was determined not to let personal feelings get in the way of any job he would be asked to do.

He was brought out of his thoughts when the horse-drawn carriage came to an abrupt stop outside a grand-looking brick building. He brushed aside the soldier who tried to help him from the carriage.

'I haven't quite reached the old bones stage yet, soldier, but I expect old Porky Stanmore has. He must be the size of an elephant by now after sitting on his fat ass all day.'

Thomas could tell that the soldier wanted to laugh, but he was glad that he didn't, because Major Linford had remained stony-faced, and Thomas didn't want to get the young soldier in to any kind of trouble.

Once they were inside the large marbled hall, Linford asked Thomas for his weapon and belt so that he could carry out the arrangements to have it serviced.

Thomas expressed his concern after he unbuckled the belt and handed it to the major. 'I hope your boys make a good job of it. I don't want it jamming on me in a tight situation. It happened to me once in Shelander County; it's one of the reasons why I limp the way I do.' Thomas slapped the side of his right knee at the spot where the bullet had entered, but Linford assured him that he need have no worries, and he passed on the belt and weapon to the soldier.

Thomas would have liked to stop and view the large paintings of American military men that lined both sides of the corridor that led to the general's office. The one at the end of the line bore the name General Stanmore. The face of the man in the resplendent uniform looked much younger than Thomas ever remembered Stanmore, even at the start of the war.

'It must be his young brother,' Thomas muttered.

'What did you say, Marshal?' Linford asked.

'I was saying he must have a proud mother. But I

expect she's passed on.'

Linford had heard what Thomas had said and this time he'd smiled, but didn't let Thomas see him.

It was the biggest room that Thomas had ever been in, except for when he'd been to church. Stanmore was seated behind a large desk that was under the window and looking like the cat that got the cream. He roared out his thanks to the major and told him to pick up Thomas in half an hour.

Thomas started the short trek to the front of the desk where he was able to get a proper look at Stanmore. It pleased him to see how awful he looked and instinctively he looked back towards the corridor where the flattering painting hung.

'Marshal Thomas, you're looking . . . well,' Stanmore said, apparently reluctant to acknowledge that the years had been kinder to Thomas than himself when he added, 'But you don't seem as mobile as you used to be, but I guess a lot of years have gone by since we last met. I was sorry to hear about what happened to your eye. Terrible business. Anyway, sit down; we've got a lot to get through. That problem with the train hasn't left much time to prepare you for the assignment.'

Thomas wished that jowl face would get on with it, and was pleased when the assignment was finally explained to him, but even more baffled as to why he had been chosen.

'So is everything clear, Marshal, or do I need to run through it again?'

'Oh, it's clear enough, but I don't understand

34

why you need me if the job is so simple and it's not dangerous. The thing is, General, I need to be back in Statton Crossing as soon as I can.'

Stanmore's face reddened even further and he puffed on his cigar, giving himself time to think. He should have known that Thomas wouldn't just do as he was ordered. The passing years hadn't taught Thomas anything about the need for obedience which was the most important aspect of military life. If Stanmore had created a motto it would have been 'Do, don't question' but he had to remember that he needed to humour the cantankerous Thomas.

'Nothing can be more important than this assignment, and that's why you were specially selected. We both know that we have had our differences in the past, but I put all those aside when I selected you personally. It's because you have a fine record of service and, because . . .' Stanmore paused and picked up the decanter. 'I haven't even offered you a drink after your long journey. Let's have a large brandy and I'll continue with my explanation.'

Thomas watched Stanmore pour the drinks with a shaking hand. He had never regarded Stanmore as the sort to dish out soft soap, but that is what he was doing now. Whatever he was going to be told, Thomas already sensed it wasn't the truth, and he'd had enough of Stanmore's bullshit.

'If I've simply got to ride into a deserted town and hand over a parcel of money then I don't see any special skills or experience being required. They let the little girl go, she walks to the waiting carriage at the end of the old Main Street and I ride back here.'

Stanmore took a gulp of brandy and then sighed. 'I didn't want to mention this to you because it's classified information, but the little girl is no ordinary girl.'

Thomas was intrigued. 'In what way?' he asked.

'She's the granddaughter of a very important person. That's as much as I can tell you. That's why it's essential that you don't try any heroics tomorrow. You'll be armed, but that's for your own protection. The swines who have kidnapped the girl will be confident that you won't try anything while she is in danger. So just follow your instructions: keep it nice and simple, and that's an order.'

'And what about back-up in case something goes wrong?' Thomas asked.

'There won't be any back-up. The girl's family want the money handed over and no action will be taken against these men. So, is it absolutely clear what you have to do?'

'I guess so,' replied Thomas, who now felt that at least it made some sense. He was there as some kind of insurance that everyone believed wouldn't be required. According to Stanmore, the girl was only ten years old and although Thomas had no children of his own, he had a soft spot for children.

'Major Linford will arrange a horse for you.'

Thomas explained that he had brought his own horse because he might have to ride back to Statton Crossing to attend to his important business.

'You won't be kept here any longer than necessary, I'll see you tomorrow for the debriefing, of course, but after that I don't expect we'll meet again with us both retiring in the next couple of years.' Stanmore was thinking that Thomas wouldn't have to worry about his damned important business for much longer, or any debriefing. It was likely that the next time they came this close together would be at Thomas's funeral in a few days' time.

FIVE

Joe and Slim were about to spend their seventh night shacked up in what remained of the Set Them Up saloon, one of the few buildings left standing in the shanty town of Old Dalham.

'What happens if Cropper doesn't show?' asked Slim.

'He'll show because he's greedy and wants the money. That's why he agreed to our plan in the first place.'

'But what if he doesn't, Joe? We won't be going back to prison if this goes wrong. They'll either hang us, or shoot us if the army are involved.'

Joe was the calmer of the two brothers who now looked more like twins since Slim had lost all his blubber after ten years of prison food and hard labour.

'I keep telling ya, nothing's going to go wrong. I was a bit worried that Cropper might turn us in to the authorities and hope for a reward. That's why his little girl is keeping that little madam company upstairs.'

Slim looked saddened. 'Yeah, but I didn't like you doing that. She's a sweet kid, not like miss snooty. Remember that Cropper is in this as much as we are and we couldn't do this without him. I didn't like him when he first came to the prison for – what did he call it? – embezzlement. That don't seem like a proper crime to me, but he's all right.'

'Look, will you stop worrying, Slim. Those kids aren't going to get hurt unless someone does something really stupid, and if they do, then it's their fault, not ours. I agree that we needed Cropper, that's why he's getting an equal share. Now let's have a game of cards, and remember, this time tomorrow we'll be rich, and better still, Thomas will be dead. Just like that lying bank manager in Bruesburg.'

Slim was a born worrier and he felt no better despite his brother's confident assurance, but he wasn't just concerned about his own welfare. He shuffled the pack of cards again and again, his thoughts still troubling him.

'Joe, if something goes wrong tomorrow, you wouldn't shoot that little girl, would you? I know she's a brat but she ain't done us any harm and she's only a kid. You said that she wouldn't come to any harm unless they messed up. You said that, didn't you?'

There was no sign of concern on Joe's face when he replied to his brother. 'Well, I might change my mind. Aren't you forgetting that our two little sisters died because of the conditions we were living in? They were no older than the kid upstairs. The politicians didn't help us none when they lived in luxury with their fine houses and fancy clothes while we were starving. Pa tried to scratch a living out of ground that saw too much sun and not enough rain. If things do go wrong then you, me, and Cropper are dead, even if we let the girl go, but I'm betting that they won't take a chance of fouling things up. Then again, maybe the kid dying might help the politicians realize that they can be hurt as well.'

The anger left Joe's face as he felt a sense of pride, realizing that his name might go down in history. He could become a folk hero. His name would be mentioned around camp-fires as the man who struck a blow for the poor people. Ordinary folks wouldn't shed a tear for a rich kid who had more money to spend on toys and fancy dresses than poor kids had for food and a pair of shoes to protect their blistered feet.

Slim was soft, always had been, but he'd make him understand when it was all over. Joe wasn't expecting to live long enough to enjoy the ransom money. He'd started coughing up blood a few weeks ago and no amount of money could fix that, but it might help him enjoy whatever time he had left.

'But do you think Thomas will come, Joe? What if he's properly armed? Remember how useful he was with a weapon.'

'Thomas will be here and if the other party have done like they were told, his weapon won't be much use to him. Now, stop worrying and deal the cards.'

The brothers played cards in comparative silence

with no more worrying questions, but Slim still had things on his mind and didn't win a single game, despite usually being the better player.

'We should have played for real money, Slim, and you could have settled up tomorrow out of your share.' Joe laughed at his suggestion, but he was only joking. He would never take advantage of his brother. They were much too close for that.

'What was that noise?' whispered Joe. It was his turn to be jumpy and both brothers had drawn their weapons by the time Norman Cropper came through the door.

'Jesus,' said Joe, 'why didn't you signal like we arranged? You're damned lucky not to be lying there dead and that little girl upstairs would have lost her daddy.'

'Sorry, I forgot. I've brought some food for you and the girls,' whispered Cropper.

'Never mind the food, have you brought any news?' Joe growled.

Cropper was obviously feeling the strain as much as Slim and he blurted out another sorry before explaining that everything was arranged. The ransom money would be delivered at ten o'clock tomorrow.

Joe was excited by the news but he wasn't celebrating just yet. 'And Marshal Thomas will be the one to deliver it?'

'Just like you asked for. My contact told me that he arrived in Dalham this afternoon. Did you know that he's only got one eye?'

Joe and Slim shook hands in celebration before

Joe replied that they had heard about the marshal losing an eye but didn't know if it was true.

'What about his weapon being crocked?' Joe asked.

'That's been arranged, but if what I was told about him is true, it wouldn't matter if he was armed, especially against two of you. He's an old man who can hardly walk and should have retired years ago.'

Slim's spirits had been lifted by the news and when Cropper went upstairs to see his daughter he spoke to his brother. 'I still think we should torture the bastard first for what he did to us. He may be a crocked old guy now, but he's had ten years of living. Ten years of sleeping with a woman every night while we rotted in that prison for something we didn't do.'

Joe smiled at Slim. 'Don't worry, Brother, you can start making up for lost time tomorrow. We can work our way through all the girls in one saloon and then move on to the next. Of course, I get to be first with each of the girls because I'm older than you.' Joe laughed, but Slim was back to being worried; this time it was over something different, but just as serious as far as he was concerned.

'Joe, do you believe all those stories about the authorities putting something into the drink that affects, you know what?'

'What do you mean by, you know what?' Joe teased, knowing full well what his brother meant.

'I mean you can't get it up in the stallion stakes, that's what I mean.'

'You won't have any difficulty, and I'll tell you why,' Joe assured his brother, and looked towards the stairs and then lowered his voice. 'We both had the same to drink in prison and I had no trouble giving it to Cropper's missus that night we stayed with them. Remember Norman gave us a lot of liquor? Well, you were out for the count and then Norman had to go and do some business. That's when I did some business myself.'

Slim grinned. 'You didn't! Mind you she's not much of a looker. She's almost as big as I was in the old days, but I did have trouble trying not to stare at those big titties of hers.'

'Never mind her looks; she was one hot lady. It's a wonder she didn't wake you up with all the noises she made, panting and moaning the way she did. I could tell she was grateful because the following morning she gave me a bigger breakfast than you and Norman.'

The brothers laughed, but Slim became serious again. 'Joe, I've been thinking about what you said about killing the kid if you have to, and it just ain't right. I'm not with you on this one.'

'Think of the effect it would have. We would be striking a blow for all the poor people, and it would make the politicians take notice for a change. It would have more impact that assassinating the president himself. It would be a sort of justice. Remember we've spent ten years in a stinking prison for something we didn't do, so why not let someone else have some of the pain?'

'Jesus Christ, Joe! We'll all end up dead if you kill

that girl. What about the money, and what about the marshal? I thought this was all about Thomas?'

'I'm not saying I'm going to kill her, but I'm thinking about it,' Joe lied.

The discussion ended when they heard Cropper coming down the stairs.

'The girls are fine,' Cropper reported. 'I've told them that they're going home tomorrow. Now I think we ought to go through what's going to happen. Remember you agreed that the girls wouldn't see any killing.'

'If that's what I said then that's what will happen,' Joe said, and then explained the plans. 'You take the money off Thomas and bring it inside. Once you've made sure that the money is correct we'll take care of Thomas. We'll let the little brat go, as soon as we've dragged the big ape out of sight. You can tell the girls that there's going to be some shooting practice.'

They discussed the details of their plans for the last time before the three men tried to sleep ahead of the day that would change their lives for better or worse, of that there was no doubt.

Joe's mind was in a whirl as he now believed that destiny had brought him here. He'd been fooling himself thinking that they could get away with it. The reward for their capture would be so high that someone would turn them in if the army or a bounty hunter didn't get them first. By the time he eventually slept he was thinking that the ideal solution tomorrow would be for him to kill Thomas and then the girl. He just hoped that when it was over he could make Slim understand.

It would be many hours after Joe fell asleep before Norman Cropper could do likewise after what he had heard the brothers discussing while he was listening at the top of the stairs when he'd gone to check on the girls. He had always had his doubts about Joe after some of the things he'd done and said while he was in prison, and now he was wishing that he hadn't got involved with them. The main thing was that at least his own little girl would be safe if he did what Joe told him, but that wouldn't stop him from being executed for his part in the kidnap.

Cropper wasn't a violent man and he had never even fired a gun in anger before, let alone killed a man, but perhaps his best chance was to kill the brothers while they were asleep. That way he could keep all the money for himself, and if he got caught he could explain that he had saved the girl's life. The problem was he would have to be absolutely certain that both the brothers were asleep before he made his move.

SIX

It was just after eight o'clock when Thomas made the short walk from the garrison canteen to the stables. Major Linford was already mounted and a soldier was holding the reins of Thomas's stallion, that was looking in better condition then ever after being groomed by one of the stable hands.

Linford gave him a nod and asked him if he'd been well fed at breakfast. Thomas made sure he had a clear view of the major's face when he replied.

'It was fine, Major. It would have been worthy of a condemned man's last meal.' If Linford knew more about the assignment than he was letting on, then he would make a good poker player because his face gave nothing away.

Linford nudged his sorrel closer to the stallion and handed Thomas a piece of paper. 'This message came through just as I was leaving HQ. It was sent from Fort Hoch by Marshal Patterson. I thought you might want to see it as soon as possible.'

46

Thomas read the short message and stuffed the paper in his pocket without commenting, but he needn't hurry back to Statton Crossing. The message had read 'Brothers in custody – no problems encountered'. He felt as though a load had been lifted off his shoulders as he rode alongside Linford towards the garrison gates.

Linford wasn't the most talkative of men, but Thomas sensed that he was nervous, and although Thomas wasn't one for small talk either, he did make a few attempts before he gave up. He was uneasy when Linford pulled up when they were a mile away from Old Dalham, and announced that this was as far as he was going. He appeared edgy when he wished Thomas well, and told him that he would see him back at the garrison when the mission was over. Thomas was still puzzled why the major had come with him unless it was to be part of the glory without taking any of the risks. It still riled Thomas that he hadn't been told the identity of the senior official whose granddaughter was being held, and he doubted if he ever would.

When Thomas reached the carriage on the edge of town he was greeted by a young captain named Jameson. The captain didn't introduce the young soldier, but Thomas found out his name was Dodson. The view of Main Street ahead brought back memories when he came here to help tackle a gang that had been terrorizing the town. He had killed one of the gang and wounded two others in a gun battle that had lasted almost an hour. It had been a bustling town then, thanks to the nearby silver mine. When the mine closed, the town died.

Captain Jameson had his eye to the long brass telescope most of the time and told Thomas that there had been no sign of activity near the saloon since he'd arrived there over an hour ago. Thomas and Dodson had been passing the time by talking about army life and they were laughing when Captain Jameson announced that it was time to go. The soft leather case containing the ransom money had already been strapped to the stallion. Thomas hadn't been told how much ransom money had been demanded, but judging by the bulging case, it must have been a tidy sum.

As Thomas moved off Dodson gave the stallion a playful pat and wished Thomas good luck and told him to be careful. Thomas eased the stallion forward and was only a few yards away when Captain Jameson shouted after him, 'Make sure the President's granddaughter is kept safe, Marshal.'

There weren't many things that would stop Thomas in his tracks, but what Jameson had just said nearly did. 'Jesus, no wonder they're all jumpy,' Thomas muttered to himself.

He didn't know whether Jameson had been told to tell him at the last minute, or if it had just slipped out. He remembered that the girl's grandfather had been described as a very important person. The word understatement came to his mind.

At least he now knew the real reason why Stanmore had picked him. It was nothing to do with any baloney about him being the best man. If things went wrong for Stanmore then he would take

Thomas down with him, or make him take all the blame.

It was always sad when a once vibrant town was reduced to what he was seeing now in the form of crumbling paintwork, broken doors and shutters, as well as the many buildings that had collapsed completely. The ones that still stood would have been looted and many folks' dreams and ambitions had died with the town. Perhaps one day, Old Dalham would become famous for what might be the most dramatic kidnap of all time.

Thomas snapped himself out of his thoughts as he reached the saloon and dismounted. He hitched the stallion to the rickety rail and wriggled his right hand to rid it of any stiffness, making sure that if he needed to use his pistol, then he was ready. The silence was broken by a voice calling out from inside the saloon, ordering him to lay the money on the steps outside the saloon and then to step back.

Thomas was thinking that he might not get to see the kidnappers when a weedy-looking guy in a city suit appeared. He didn't look like the sort to mastermind a job like this on his own and for a brief moment he thought it was Henry Tyler, the confidence trickster. A closer look revealed this man to be even thinner: his moustache was bushier and he was armed, although judging by the way the holster was twisted around, it didn't look like he was used to firing it. And in contrast to Tyler doing business, this man was as jumpy as a rabbit as he snatched the ransom case and then retreated inside.

While Thomas waited for the next move, he

surveyed the scene to see if there was any sign that the jumpy one might have an accomplice. Whoever was involved in this must have come here by horse, but there were no tell-tale signs that a horse had been near the front of the saloon recently. He'd already noted that the livery building was almost flattened, so it was most likely that their animals were behind the saloon.

When the man reappeared, he was still looking nervous when he spoke to Thomas. 'You can go. We'll send the girl out when you are halfway down Main Street.'

Thomas studied the thin features of the man, hoping that he might get to meet him again, but he was relieved that things appeared to be progressing well. The man had said 'we'll send the girl out' indicating that he wasn't acting alone. Thomas had turned the stallion to face towards the far end of Main Street where the carriage was waiting and was about to put his foot in the stirrup when a voice called out.

'Not so fast, Marshal.'

Thomas turned around slowly, to see that the 'jumpy' one had gone and two men who had been on his mind until this morning were standing in front of the saloon. The newlook Slim was grinning, but Joe looked as mean as ever. Thomas was wondering who was locked up in a cell in Statton Crossing, because it wasn't the Carter brothers, but at least the town was safe from them.

'I heard that you were out, boys, but I didn't think threatening little girls was your style,' said

Thomas, who was surprised, but unruffled.

'We ain't got a style, Marshal, because we ain't ever done anything wrong until now,' Joe Carter snapped.

'Except kill that bank manager last week,' Slim reminded his brother, and then added, 'Remember him, Marshal? You and him got us sent to prison for something that we didn't do.'

Thomas had always harboured some doubts about the brothers being guilty of robbing the bank in Bruesburg, but it had not caused him any lost sleep. He was certain that they had done other robberies, and anyway he had only arrested them on suspicion; it was the jury and the judge who sent them to jail.

'If what you say is true, then I'm real sorry if a miscarriage of justice has taken place,' Thomas said with a little sympathy.

Joe was angered by the coolness of the marshal who did not appear to be showing any signs of fear, but he would if he knew that his trusted weapon was now useless.

'Sorry, ain't good enough, Marshal, but we're fair-minded men, and seeing how there are two of us you can go for your gun first.'

'Let the little girl go, like you promised,' Thomas said.

'Did we promise that? Sorry, no can do,' Joe replied, clearly enjoying the encounter. 'That kid's going out of here the same way you are. All stiff, tied to a horse, or in an undertaker's box. Now, let's cut out the chin-wagging and get this over with.'

Thomas had been slowly edging his way around so that when he drew his pistol he would be best placed to shoot Joe first, and he also wanted to get the stallion out of the line of fire. He'd figured that Joe would be the faster of the two, but it was Slim who was only a fraction slower than Thomas in drawing his weapon. Joe was the first to fall from the impact of Thomas's first shot and then Slim quickly followed his brother on to the dust of Main Street. The bullet that had ended Slim's worrying hadn't come from Thomas's gun, but from the one that Norman Cropper had just thrown to the ground outside the saloon.

'I'm not armed, Marshal. I'm coming out with my hands up,' Cropper called out, still surprised that he had found the courage that he had lacked last night when he was thinking about tackling the brothers while they slept.

Thomas's priority was the safety of the girl, but it only needed a glance at the brothers to realize that the services of a hangman wouldn't be required.

'If anything's happened to the girl you'll be join-ing your friends, mister, and that's a promise,' Thomas threatened.

'She's upstairs with my own girl, Belle, and she's safe. I didn't want anything to do with the girl being killed, that's why I shot Slim Carter. I swear I didn't want anything to happen to her.'

'You'd best save your pleading for the jury. Now lie on the ground, face down next to those sorry specimens, while I go and check on the girls. If you're thinking of trying to escape, remember that half the United States Army will come after you.'

Thomas holstered his gun and then picked up Cropper's pistol that had landed near the Carter brothers and then made sure that Cropper had his face in the dust before he left him. Thomas found the two girls in a small room upstairs, sitting on a bed surrounded by toys and neither looking distressed by the experience. The slightly older girl who asked him if the men had finished target practice was obviously the President's granddaughter. She had an air of confidence that wasn't found in ordinary kids.

'There won't be any more gunfire, I promise you,' Thomas replied, without directly answering her question and then added, 'There'll be a carriage arriving soon to take you home, but until then you'd best stay up here.' Thomas tried to be as gentle as he could, but he wasn't used to dealing with children.

When Thomas was back outside the saloon he waved his arms in a prearranged signal for the carriage to come forward, and then questioned the jumpy one, who told him that his name was Norman Cropper.

Thomas sighed heavily when Cropper had finished his account of things. 'You're in serious trouble, Cropper. The way you acted at the end might just help save your life, but I wouldn't count on it. I suppose if you hadn't have shot Slim Carter in the back he might have got the better of me, then who knows what tragedy might have followed. There's no telling what Slim might have done to avenge his brother's death.'

Captain Jameson had a face like thunder, and accused Thomas of fouling up the operation. Thomas didn't take kindly to being bawled out and made that clear to Jameson, after he'd told him that the girl was safe and none the worse for the experience.

'The feller on the ground is Norman Cropper who was in on the kidnap, but he helped me by killing one of the varmints,' said Thomas, nodding towards Cropper. 'The problem is that his little girl is upstairs with the President's granddaughter. Apparently it was the Carter brothers' idea of insurance in case Cropper ratted on them. If Dodson gives me a hand, we can move the bodies out of sight, and then the girls can come down and you can transport both the girls back to Dalham. I'll find out from Cropper where the girl lives. I'll take Cropper back to the garrison's prison block.'

Captain Jameson didn't like Thomas taking charge the way he had, but he went along with it, although he made Thomas aware that Major Linford might not be completely satisfied with things.

'You might want to tell the major that this was some kind of set-up to get at me, but I guess the major and Stanmore already know that. You can also tell them that Joe Carter planned to kill the child as well.'

Jameson didn't comment and Thomas set about moving the bodies with Dodson. Thomas was amused at the way the young soldier avoided looking at the Carter brothers when they carried them into the rundown barber's shop that was next to the saloon. Thomas had seen more than his fair share of faces drained of blood, and lifeless eyes that were locked in a haunting stare. He hoped that young Dodson wouldn't get to see many more bodies, but he doubted if that would be the case in this violent land. They kicked sand over the patches of blood that had leaked from the bodies making the way clear for the girls to be brought down. When Thomas told Cropper that he could speak to his daughter before she was taken back to Dalham, Captain Jameson looked as though he was about to object, but perhaps the glare from Thomas made him change his mind.

Major Linford was waiting at the guard-room when Thomas arrived back at the garrison with Cropper, and he ordered two soldiers to take Cropper to the prison block. The major's congratulation lacked any real conviction, and he appeared troubled by something despite the success of the operation, and Thomas wondered what it might be.

Linford's mood didn't improve when they got to Stanmore's office and found that Captain Jameson was already there updating the general on what had happened. At least Stanmore appeared in good spirits when he greeted them. He addressed Linford when he said that he had been asked by the President's office to convey his thanks to all the military personnel who had taken part in the operation. There was no direct acknowledgment of

Thomas's role before Stanmore said it was time to get down to business.

'Captain Jameson has given me most of the details about the three men involved and I'm sure when we interrogate this fellow Cropper we'll find out more. So if we can just run through what happened at Old Dalham, then you can provide me with a written report within the hour. I expect you'll be leaving us then, Marshal Thomas.'

'As soon as I can, General,' he replied, silently cursing Stanmore for his apparent liking of red tape and paperwork.

'Right, then let's get on. I think the only item we need to cover here is the sequence of events that led to the deaths of the two men. So, if you would like to give us your version, Marshal.'

Thomas didn't like Stanmore's inference. 'There's only one version, General. The Carter brothers intended to kill me, but I think you might have known that all along. They called me out and seemed confident that they would get the better of me. I managed to get a shot off at Joe Carter which proved fatal and then Cropper had a pang of conscience and shot Slim Carter in the back.'

Stanmore smiled when he said, 'So it was just as well that you had your weapon fully serviced before you left, even though you weren't expecting to use it. I guess you know now why you were chosen for this assignment. Joe Carter made it part of their demands, but I was confident that you could handle them.' Thomas noted that the general was looking at Linford when he made his last remark. Thomas

56

wanted to say that if someone hadn't slipped a note under his door last night and warned him to rearm his weapon then he wouldn't be standing here now. Thomas had replaced the bullets in the chamber from the box of spares he had in his travelling bag. He had even taken the precaution of firing off a test round before he'd gone to breakfast. Thomas considered raising the matter of the tampered weapon, but figured that any enquiry into it might delay his departure, and he didn't want that. He also feared that if Stanmore found out about the warning, then the career of the person who had warned Thomas would be over. Stanmore wasn't just an incompetent bully, he was vindictive.

'Of course, you were taking a chance that the operation could have ended in failure if they had got the better of you. Perhaps they never intended to kill you; you did admit that you were the first to draw a weapon.'

Thomas could feel his blood temperature rising. 'I wasn't about to play guessing games with them, especially Joe. Anyway, why are we having this post-mortem? Hasn't the captain informed you that Cropper told me that Joe Carter was going to kill the girl as well? What more proof do you want that they wanted more than just the ransom money?'

Stanmore smiled. 'Ah, yes, Cropper. I don't believe his story. I think he was actually trying to shoot at you, and hit Carter in the back. I'm sure that's what the prosecution will say at his trial, and he won't escape a hanging.'

'You can think what you like, General, but I

believe that he's telling the truth and I'll make sure I say so in my report,' Thomas snapped, wishing that this farce would end soon before he really lost his temper with Stanmore.

Stanmore frowned, and was clearly upset with Thomas. 'You must do as you wish, Marshal. Now I just need to hear Major Linford's account, but there's no need for you or the captain to be present, so you can go and get on with writing your reports.'

Thomas and Captain Jameson were dismissed without any further congratulations and Thomas suspected that Stanmore was getting ready to milk any praise that would be forthcoming from government officials.

Thomas was putting the finishing touches to his report when he received the first of two callers to his room at the garrison. Major Linford was not entirely unexpected, nor was what he said. He advised Thomas not to include any opinions about Cropper in his report and to let things ride, claiming that Cropper would get his chance to put his own case at his trial.

'You're too late, Major, because I've already included it, and even if I hadn't, I wouldn't have left it out. It's my report and I'll write it my way. And in case you and the general are worried about me mentioning that my pistol was interfered with, you needn't worry. I haven't included that but I might still take it up with the general.'

'What are you suggesting, Marshal?' Linford asked.

'Look, Major, I haven't got time for games. If you say that you don't know about anyone tampering with my Peacemaker, then fine. Let's leave it there. But you can tell me whose idea it was to have my pistol overhauled.'

Linford hesitated before he replied. 'Actually, it was General Stanmore's idea. I think he was just being professional. He didn't want to leave anything to chance in case something went wrong. I still don't understand your concern, Marshal, especially after the weapon didn't let you down.'

'I think we should drop this, Major. Now I need to finish this report.'

'Very well, I'll leave you to get on with it, and in case we don't meet again, I wish you well. And once again, congratulations on a fine piece of work today.'

Linford shook hands with Thomas and left, leaving Thomas unsure about his involvement. But he was certain that Linford was working for Stanmore and he didn't trust either man.

When Thomas heard the second knock on the door, he thought it would be Linford who had forgotten to mention something. Instead, he opened the door to see the smiling face of General Claud T. Mosley, the most senior officer at Dalham Garrison, accompanied by a tall man in a city suit and starched collar. Thomas wasn't usually over-awed by top brass, but he was on this occasion. General Mosley was everything that Stanmore wasn't, and a fine soldier.

'I understand that you're about to leave us,

Marshal,' Mosley said, 'but I would like you to delay your departure for just a short while. I'm sure you'll agree to let the Vice President of the United States convey the President's thanks to you in person for what you did today.'

Thomas was lost for words, a point picked up on by General Mosley who gave a broad smile. 'I take it that your silence means that you accept the invitation. So, if you would like to come with us now and receive the thanks you deserve. By the way, this is Mr Horrocks the Vice-President's personal secretary. He'll acquaint you with the procedure on our way to the governor's house the other side of the city. I'll arrange for you to be brought back here after you've seen the Vice President.'

On the way to the government building, General Mosley explained that the Vice President was a no-nonsense, down-to-earth character, who especially wanted to see the man who was involved in the actual action today. Thomas wondered how red Stanmore's face would get when he found out that Thomas had been given the VIP treatment. Thomas wasn't one for being made a fuss over, but it would be a bonus if it upset General Stanmore.

When Thomas left the magnificent office that made Stanmore's looked ordinary, he was feeling a sense of pride that made his job worthwhile. The Vice President was no bullshitter, and was obviously a busy man, so his personal thanks during their brief meeting were much appreciated.

*

It was late afternoon by the time Thomas delivered his report to Stanmore's admin officer. He also used the opportunity to send a message off to Marshal Patterson, telling him that the Carter brothers were dead, and suggested that he release the two men who were being held. He also added that he would be riding back to Statton Crossing. According to the map he'd seen at the garrison, the journey to Lake Yuset seemed straightforward. Once he got to the lake he was familiar with the rest of the trail to Statton Crossing.

He had been riding for less than an hour when the trail ended at the banks of a river, but all that remained of the bridge were the supports. When his cursing stopped, he tossed a coin to decide which way he would go along the bank that ran west to east, hoping to find another crossing that would take him north. His instinct told him west, and after he'd finished his rye bread and beef supplied by the cook-house sergeant, he decided to ignore the result of the coin toss and follow his nose.

Thomas was fuming again an hour later when there was still no sign of a crossing. He'd made frequent stops to test the depth of the river with a long branch that he'd snapped off one of the cottonwood trees growing near the bank, but it was too deep to attempt a crossing.

By the time the sun was beginning to sit low in the sky he realized that he had made a mistake because he was now at the point where he was heading further away from his destination. He had no way of knowing just how close he was to finding a crossing so he turned his horse, intending to back-track and then head the way that the coin had chosen for him.

He had travelled barely a hundred yards when he saw the two riders coming in his direction. The two soldiers riding side by side were certainly in a hurry, but Thomas intended to make sure that they stopped long enough to tell him where to cross the river. He was pleased when they started to rein in their mounts, but had serious doubts that they would want to help him, because the sergeant was pointing a pistol at him.

'Get off your horse, nice and slow, Marshal,' the sergeant ordered.

Thomas had been thinking that it was a simple case of mistaken identity, but being addressed as Marshal had just removed that likelihood.

'I'm not moving until you tell why you're point-ing that weapon at me,' Thomas said in defiant mood, thinking that the presence of the two soldiers must have something to do with earlier events that day. He wondered who had sent the men after him, and why.

'We've been ordered to take you into custody and that's what we aim to do,' growled the sergeant. 'Now you can either co-operate or make life diffi-cult for yourself. It don't matter none to us because we intend to carry out our orders. Now what's it going to be?'

Thomas was more angry than concerned despite the gun being directed at him, but he didn't see any point in making matters worse and he started to dismount. 'Right, I'll go along with this, but when I've cleared this up, I suggest that you stay out of my way.'

'I don't think we'll be seeing much of each other, Marshal. Now just ease your gunbelt off, pass it to the soldier and then you can remount,' ordered the sergeant. He waited until the weapon was safely in the hands of the soldier and then he removed Thomas's rifle from its holder on the stallion.

Thomas froze as the sergeant primed the rifle ready for use and then fired off three shots into the air, to signal the other search party that he had been arrested. During the ride back to the garrison, Thomas was flanked by the two soldiers, neither of whom uttered a word. He had considered that his arrest might be some part of a hoax to get him back for another presentation, but he doubted if the dumb sergeant could play act so well. No, this was for real, and it was serious.

As the garrison came into view he recalled that it was only hours earlier that he had left feeling like some kind of hero. He wondered what Norman Cropper would make of it all if they ended up in adjoining cells.

SEVEN

Thomas had been resting on the bed in the tiny cell for more than an hour when he heard the rattle of keys. One of the officers entering his cell was Major Linford, but the young lieutenant wasn't familiar to him, nor was the guard who was clearly intent on keeping a watchful eye on him.

Linford was grim-faced when he spoke to Thomas after he had introduced Lieutenant Anderson who had been assigned to represent him. 'If you take my advice, you'll plead guilty and save everyone a lot of trouble.'

Thomas's face reddened, but he controlled himself when he replied to Linford, 'I might, if someone would tell me what the hell I'm supposed to have done.'

Linford looked annoyed. 'There are a lot of very angry people here at the garrison and you are not going to help matters by denying that you murdered General Stanmore. Everyone knows that you didn't like him, but you must have had a bout of insanity to do such a horrible thing, and on what should have been a day of celebration for us all after the success of the mission.'

Thomas, had considered many possibilities as to why he had been dragged back to the garrison and settled on the most likely one being that something had been stolen and he was a suspect. But he could never have imagined that he would be accused of murder.

'That's about the craziest thing I have ever heard. I won't deny that I disliked the man, but I'm not in the habit of killing people just because I don't like them. I'm sorry to hear that the general's dead.'

Linford sighed. 'You obviously don't intend to be co-operative so let's get the formalities over.' Linford straightened up and almost came to attention as he continued in a formal tone, 'Marshal Thomas, you are being held for the murder of General Stanmore in his office shortly before you left the garrison this afternoon.'

When the news had sunk in, Thomas could understand that he would be an obvious suspect. Stanmore must have been disliked by many people, but they hadn't made their feelings known like he had.

'But I didn't see the general again after I left the debriefing that you were at, so I had no opportunity to kill him, not that I wanted to,' was all he could say.

Linford hadn't been involved in something like this before and he was eager to extract himself from the situation as soon as possible and made his final remarks to Thomas. 'You need to talk things through with the lieutenant. He's the man you'll need to convince if you insist on claiming your innocence. But the evidence that I've heard looks pretty damning. Now I'll leave you to it.'

Thomas had already decided the fresh-faced lieutenant must have been barely out of law school and not the ideal choice for someone whose life might depend on his skills.

'No offence, son, but are you the best they could offer me?' Thomas asked.

Lieutenant Anderson waited until Linford was clear of the cells before he spoke and when he did, he ignored Thomas's question and surprised him on two counts. Firstly, because his voice was deep and firm, and secondly, he told Thomas that he believed that he was innocent.

'I bet you say that to all your clients,' replied Thomas, with a mixture of cynicism and humour.

Anderson smiled, but there was no trace of embarrassment when he replied, 'I can vouch that's not so, Marshal, because I've never had any other clients. You will be my first, unless you ask for someone else.'

Thomas forgot the seriousness of his plight and laughed. 'Jesus, son, they don't intend for you to get off to a winning start. Then again I won't be the first innocent man to be found guilty. In fact, two such men died this morning, and if it wasn't for them I wouldn't be in this predicament now, but that's another story.'

Anderson had already warmed to the man who had been accused of ripping out General

Stanmore's throat. He believed that the marshal would hang no matter who defended him, but he hoped that somehow he could beat the odds and save him.

'Why don't I go through the procedures,' Anderson suggested, 'and then I'll outline the details of the case against you. If after that you feel that you would like someone else, then I'll report that back to my office and they'll assign another attorney. How does that sound?'

Thomas rubbed his chin and hesitated before he replied. 'Fair enough, but you ought to know that I hated Stanmore's guts and I ain't going to deny that in any court.'

'I know, and that's one of the reasons why I think you're innocent,' Anderson said, hoping to give Thomas some encouragement.

Anderson started by saying that Thomas's obvious dislike of the general was well known, but Thomas interrupted him. 'They can't hang a man because he doesn't like someone.'

'But they can if his knife is found next to the body and he was the last known person to see the victim.'

Thomas sighed and said, 'So that's what happened to my bowie knife.'

'So, you're not denying that the murder weapon could belong you?'

'My knife isn't exactly a custom model. I noticed it missing when I wanted to use it to hack off a cottonwood branch shortly before I was arrested by the soldiers. I had it when I returned from the kidnap incident this morning, but it could have been taken from my saddle-bag by someone.'

'You told Major Linford that you hadn't seen the general again after the debriefing, but according to his admin officer, Captain Craddock, you handed him your report and then asked to see the general.'

If Thomas had any doubts that he was in trouble they had just been removed.

'I did, but I didn't see him,' Thomas said, realizing how flimsy his explanation was going to sound.

'Captain Craddock said that he gave you permission to see the general who was on his own, and watched you head off in the direction of the general's office. Was the general already dead when you got there? Perhaps you panicked and just left.'

'I ain't the sort to panic, son. The truth is I got to the door and raised my hand to knock, and then changed my mind. I suspected that the general might have put me in danger by having my pistol tampered with even though he knew that the Carter brothers were out to get me. I was going to have it out with him, or at least let him know that I knew about it. I take it that you know about the Carter brothers and the kidnap?'

Anderson replied that he had been briefed about the kidnap, but had already been told that it would not be allowed to be discussed in court because of the publicity ban being placed on it. Anderson was having his first doubts about Thomas's story and pressed him on his reasons for not seeing Stanmore. 'So, why did you change your mind about seeing the general? You don't seem the sort of man who would pull away from a confrontation over something so important?'

'I guess I decided that it just wasn't worthwhile and I might have thought that it would sour the success with the mission. I doubted if I would get any satisfaction out of Stanmore. He was as slippery as a barrelful of eels. So I just walked away.'

'So why didn't Captain Craddock see you leave after you'd changed your mind about seeing the general? Craddock says that he was there for another ten minutes after you had headed off to see him.'

Thomas couldn't offer an explanation, and he couldn't remember where Craddock was when he passed by the desk on his way out.

When Anderson left the cell an hour later, he had realized that he would be fighting a lost cause. Thomas had motive, opportunity, and wouldn't have been afraid of ripping out a man's throat. Anderson was no longer convinced that he would be defending an innocent man, but he would still try his damnedest to get him off.

EIGHT

It was exactly six weeks after Thomas's arrest when his trial began in the specially arranged courthouse at Dalham Garrison. The trial had been delayed because of a legal dispute as to whether Thomas should face a court martial or a civilian trial. Some legal experts argued that Thomas was a government official employed by the military, but he was by definition, a civilian. Following a great deal of legal wrangling, the military won the right to make him face a court martial, but agreed that his punishment would come under civilian administration. This meant that if he was found guilty he would face a civilian execution, or be imprisoned in a civilian jail. The terms of Thomas's punishment were regarded as academic because there was only one punishment for what he was charged with, and that was a death sentence.

There had never been any doubt in Thomas's mind that he would stick with Anderson as his defence counsel, and he had come to like him. Thomas had no expectation of getting off and he had tried to make it clear to Anderson that he shouldn't feel responsible if the verdict went against him. He really wanted to say when rather than if. The only mistake that Anderson made was not to request that General Mosley gave evidence before the general was appointed as the head of the court. General Mosley had never been a supporter of Stanmore's methods and he could have proved a useful character witness for Thomas, but that opportunity had been lost with his appointment to the court martial.

The trial was attended by some reporters from the major Eastern newspapers who had been given special permission to sit in court. They were intrigued by the idea that a man who had such an outstanding record would do such a thing, especially when he was nearing the end of such a distinguished career. More than one had carried the headline 'Killer Hero'. Although the details of the kidnap had never been revealed to the Press or public at large, many of his other heroic deeds had been published.

Thomas was being led into the courthouse when one reporter from New York shouted at him, 'Why did you do it, Marshal?'

Anderson told Thomas to ignore the caller, but Thomas paused long enough to give the reporter a scowl and to mime the words. 'You little piece of shit.'

Major John Covell, the prosecuting counsel looked bored with the proceedings from the start. Thomas had already decided that he didn't like the short, smarmy-looking character who had the easy job of getting him hanged. Covell's bulbous nose was an act of nature and not from fighting. At no more than five foot two he was about the shortest man Thomas had ever seen and he appeared to have some sort of skin disease which made him scratch his face frequently. Perhaps the rash had been brought on by nerves because Covell had downed a good deal of water from the jug in front of him before he had been invited to open his case by General Mosley.

'This is the fifteenth time that I have had the privilege of being prosecution counsel for the United States Army,' Covell said, scratched his face, and then continued, 'But this case is different from the others in two respects. Firstly, it is the most despicable, involving the cold-blooded murder of a national hero, for that is what General Stanmore was. Secondly, there is not the slightest doubt that the accused is guilty.'

Covell paused again to scratch his face, and then looked towards the members of the panel who were seated behind the table on the raised platform, giving them a commanding view of the courthouse. He held his gaze on each of the men before moving to the next. It was as though he wanted to make sure that his opening remarks had fully registered with Colonel Henry Palmer, General Mosley and Colonel Samuel Bodine.

Covell's hand had a slight tremor as he poured water from the jug and then placed the glass to his lips before continuing. 'This case is also tragic for another reason other than the loss of a great soldier and servant of our fine country. It is sad that the accused has blotted a distinguished career by taking the life of a man because of some misguided jealousy and an intense dislike of officers. The accused has carried a chip on his shoulder for most of his life and that is why he is here today facing this most serious of charges.'

Covell then outlined the prosecution case before he called Thomas to the stand where he was ordered to take the oath before Covell launched his cross examination.

'Marshal Thomas.' Covell paused deliberately in an attempt to cause Thomas some discomfort as he waited to be addressed, but discovered that he was wasting his time when Thomas gazed around the court, showing no sign of impatience or irritation. 'Marshal Thomas,' Covell repeated, 'Did you like General Stanmore?'

'No, but I didn't kill him.'

'I think we'll soon prove that you did,' Covell smirked, and then picked up the knife from the desk. 'Is this your knife?' Covell asked.

'It might be, but if you give me a closer look I could tell you for certain.'

Covell hesitated for a moment and then asked one of the guards to hand the knife to Thomas. Thomas turned the knife over to inspect both sides of the blade and then gave the knife back to the guard.

'Yep, that's my knife. There's a nick on the blade

that was caused when it struck the barrel of a gun that belonged to a feller who was intent on shooting me. It happened in a saloon in Yunkat County a couple of years back.'

Covell smiled with satisfaction, and Lt. Anderson shook his head in dismay fearing that Thomas's honesty had just removed one of the main points that he was going to cite, namely that the knife was such a common type that it could have belonged to a number of people at the garrison.

The murmurings around the court that had resulted from Thomas's admission about the owner-ship of the murder weapon stopped when Covell asked Thomas what he thought of General Stanmore.

'He was a brave man,' Thomas replied, but shat-tered Anderson's brief moment of relief, when he continued, 'but as a soldier he was about as useful as a chocolate coffee pot. General Stanmore caused the loss of many fine soldiers because of his arro-gance and stupidity.'

Covell was thinking that Thomas was either an incredibly honest man or a stupid one, but it didn't matter which it was as he drove home the point that he wanted to make.

'So, even if you hadn't murdered the general you would have been pleased to hear the news that he was dead? You would have thought that he had got what he deserved?'

'I've never taken any pleasure hearing about the loss of a human life, so it wasn't good news.'

Covell was disappointed with the answer so he

pressed on. 'According to your records, you have killed many times and there may have been others that have gone unrecorded. You would have been more capable than most men to run a knife across the general's jugular vein. In fact, you even trained men in the art of silent killing; isn't that so?'

General Mosley had been becoming more and more irritated by the line of questioning and decided to call a halt to it. 'Major Covell, the marshal has nothing to be ashamed of for carrying out lawful killings in the line of duty and I for one will not be regarding such activities as any kind of case against him. It might interest you to know that I have also had the misfortune to have found it necessary to take a human life. I might also add that I was not an admirer of all that General Stanmore did throughout his career.' Covell was clearly embarrassed by the rebuke and he immediately declared that he had no further questions.

Anderson made a determined effort to try and let Thomas expand on some of the things that he'd said but realized that Thomas's only hope was that he would be seen as a truly honest man. Anderson had been told that he was forbidden from making any references to the kidnapping and the accusation made by Thomas that his gun had been tampered with. Thomas's dislike of Stanmore was clearly seen as a motive. His own weapon had been used for the killing, and Captain Craddock had testified that Thomas had lied when he had claimed that he hadn't seen the general shortly before leaving the garrison.

During General Mosley's closing comments before the panel considered the verdict, he suggested that Thomas's life of violence while in service to his country may have disturbed his mind. Mosley's remarks might have drawn sympathy from some, but there wasn't a single person in the court who was surprised when a verdict of guilty was delivered after the briefest of discussions by the panel. There was no protest from Thomas, only a dignified acceptance that the law wasn't perfect and that telling the truth wasn't always good enough.

NINE

Five weeks after the trial there had still been no announcement of when Thomas's execution would be carried out and he had been detained in the garrison prison block. Thomas remained philosophical about it all. He even convinced himself that perhaps dying at his age wasn't such a bad thing. His life had been filled with action, and some would even say adventure. All that would have come to an end soon when Mother Nature took its course. He'd been fooling himself with his dreams of lazy days beside the river catching fish. It would have driven him mad in no time at all.

It was the following week when Lt. Anderson brought him the news that someone in high places had ordered that his death sentence be reduced to life in prison. Anderson was obviously thrilled with the news and Thomas did his best to appear pleased, despite still having the same thoughts about it being time that he left this life. He shook Anderson's hand, 'Thanks, son, I appreciate all that you have tried to do for me. Did they say what prison I'm being sent to?'

'I forgot to mention that in my excitement. You'll be going to Yukron Valley State Penitentiary tomorrow. I'm afraid I don't know much about the place except I believe its one of the oldest prisons.'

Thomas could have told Anderson all about Yukron Valley. He'd escorted prisoners there on two occasions and it was about the closest that a man could get to Hell without falling into the furnace.

Anderson was at the garrison prison when Deputy Marshal Jewson and his assistant, Symes, arrived to escort Thomas to Yukron Valley Prison. Anderson promised to take care of the sale of the stallion and Thomas was sad when he mounted the sorrel for the ride to the prison, knowing that it might be the last horse he would ever ride.

Jewson seemed a decent enough sort and once they were clear of the garrison he ordered Symes to remove the ropes securing Thomas's wrists. Perhaps Jewson thought they would get to Yukron sooner if the wrists were free, but he was hardly taking a risk with him and Symes riding either side of the prisoner.

It was late afternoon of the second day when Jewson signalled that they would make a last stop and then push on to make it to the prison before dark. It was at the end of the break as Jewson was applying the ropes to Thomas's wrists when he offered him some advice. 'You'll need to watch out for Ty Motton, the head guard. He's an evil bastard; some say he's even sadistic. He has a thing about picking on former lawmen, so you could be in line for some special treatment. So be on your guard.'

Thomas appreciated Jewson's warning and didn't tell him that he already knew of Motton's violent reputation. Nor did he mention that he'd clashed with Motton over the ill-treatment of a prisoner whom he had delivered to Yukron.

When they entered the valley, Jewson signalled for them to make a stop, and he helped Symes bind the horses' legs with sacking to help reduce the chance of snake bites which was just one of the perils on the barren plain. It was Symes's first trip to the prison and after he'd remounted, he quipped, 'I think someone must have stolen the "Welcome to Hell" sign.'

There had been plans to close the prison a few years ago after the supply wagon had been unable to cross the valley after prolonged desert storms. By the time they got the wagon through, some prisoners had died from lack of food and water. It had been decided that the prison would stay open, and an extra water-storage tank was built, as well as arrangements put in hand for increased stocks of food. During the previous year a railway line had been installed that ran for a mile to the west of the prison and after it had become operational, Motton had obtained a number of poisonous snakes from a breeder and released them into the area. The man had also supplied him with a number of mongooses imported from Asia.

The introduction of the train had taken place since Thomas's last visit and he was surprised when

Jewson directed him to the small wooden cabin next to the railway line. Thomas didn't know much about locomotives, but the faded gold and black engine wouldn't have looked out of place in a museum. There was a single carriage and three open-top wagons, one of which was loaded with supplies.

'This is as far as we take you, Marshal. The carriage is only used for top brass and prison officers. You'll be riding on one of the goods wagons so make sure you don't get too close to the edge of the open waggon. According to Motton, the stories about the snakes around here aren't exaggerated and some prisoners have died before they reached the prison, because they haven't heeded the warning.'

Thomas had just been helped down from his mount by Symes when the cabin door opened and Ty Motton appeared. He didn't look too happy, but he rarely did.

'You're late, Jewson,' Motton barked. 'I expect you've been having a few picnics with Thomas.' The notorious head guard didn't look at Thomas as he carried on complaining about being kept waiting.

Motton resembled Thomas in appearance, except that he had two eyes and the nose leaned to the right and he was slightly shorter. Despite being no stranger to brawling, he still had nearly all of his teeth, but most of them were yellow.

'Give me the papers to sign and I'll take the prisoner off your hands. There's plenty of grub in the cabin. And I expect you know all about the safety warnings regarding our slippery friends. They don't usually come too near the cabin on account of the mongooses around here, but I still advise you to keep the windows shut.'

Once the handover papers had been signed, Jewson and Symes led the three horses off to the small stable near the cabin without another word to Thomas. Motton wasn't in a talkative mood either when he drew his pistol and gestured for Thomas to walk towards one of the open waggons that were fitted with wooden seats. At least there was a sympathetic look from the train driver after he emerged from the cabin and passed Thomas on the way to the engine.

Thomas took Jewson's advice and positioned himself in the middle of the wagon because Thomas was no stranger to the tales about the snakes. He was also remembering the time that he'd been sick for a week after being bitten by a rattler in Arizona. It was about the closest he'd ever come to dying and, at the time, he'd wished he had.

Motton smiled at Thomas, aware of the precaution he had just taken. 'Don't tell me the famous marshal is frightened of a little wriggler. I had you down as having more balls.'

As the train chugged its way towards the prison, Thomas was wondering if he would ever get to ride this train again. It would be a ride to freedom if he did. He was facing towards the engine with his back to the covered carriage which was occupied by Motton, not wishing to risk seeing the sniggering features of the man who would be relishing every moment.

The surrounding scenery was not what he would have chosen to be his last view of the outside world. He spotted an odd assortment of bones, not knowing whether they were human or not, but in some cases the skeleton only had two legs.

He would have been content for the train journey to have lasted longer despite the miserable surroundings, but the train was soon coming to a halt outside the entrance to a compound that formed part of the prison. One guard was struggling to open the gate to the compound while two others, one of them holding a rifle, climbed on to the waggon and sat on the wooden seats opposite Thomas. Neither of them spoke and one seemed uninterested in their new prisoner while the other one attempted to stare Thomas out, but failed. The guard then coughed and spat on to the floor of the wagon.

Thomas smiled and said, 'You want to get a doc look at that cough, mister. You might have a serious sickness that causes you to spit like that.'

'He sounds real concerned for your health, Fletcher,' the other guard said, grinning as he did.

Fletcher had a face like thunder and snapped back at his fellow guard, 'You shut your mouth, Roper. This ugly, one-eyed freak will be worrying about his own health soon enough, and if he speaks to me again without permission, he'll be missing a tongue, as well as an eye.'

The compound gate was finally opened and the train moved inside before coming to an abrupt halt, causing Thomas to lurch forward towards the guards opposite him. Roper reacted instinctively and crashed the butt of the rifle into Thomas's face, fearing that Thomas was about to jump him. Roper's actions didn't go down too well with Fletcher, who looked down at the unconscious Thomas and growled, 'What the hell did you do that for? Now we'll have to carry the big ape to his cell.'

Thomas's nose was throbbing and he could taste blood in his mouth when he came to, and discovered that he had been laid on a thin mattress. He could still feel the rocky floor of the cell which wasn't fit for a dog, but might be his home for the rest of his life.

The cell measured eight feet by five with no ventilation except for a tiny grill in the cell door which was a spy hole to enable the guard to view the prisoner, and not out of any concern for the prisoner's health. A crumpled pile of dirty blankets lay in the corner and the paint was peeling off the walls which contained faded stains that looked like blood. Thomas hoped that they were blood, but the smell in the cell made him think of something else. The bucket that was almost filled to the brim with a dark-brown liquid was certainly the main cause of the foul stench.

Thomas had closed his eyes again when he heard footsteps and then a familiar voice. 'Welcome to the Hotel Yukron,' Motton sneered, as he entered the unlocked cell. 'One of the guards explained that you fell when the train stopped. I was going to say, be careful next time, but there won't be a next time for you.'

Thomas was having trouble trying to focus on the figure of Motton, but slowly his features came into view. Thomas sat up and spat the blood from his mouth on to the floor. His movement caused Motton to take a step back in case Thomas tried something, even though he looked all done in from the effects of the blow.

'The guard will explain the routine for emptying the piss pot. As you can see, the last occupant was a lazy bastard, but at least he managed to kill himself yesterday, or maybe he got himself killed. Either way, no one is going to mourn his loss, but you can watch him being buried later.'

Thomas's hands were free and he was thinking whether he shouldn't just give Motton a good beating and damn the consequences. The way he felt at the moment perhaps he should just kill the bastard, and then he really would face a hanging, or at least some form of death.

'You haven't got much to say for yourself, have you, Marshal? Not like last time when you started whining about a poor prisoner being treated rough. Perhaps you forgot that he molested his own daughter, but you needn't worry about him because he ain't with us anymore. No, it wasn't me who caused his little accident: that was arranged by some of his fellow prisoners.'

Thomas hoped that Motton would cut out the yapping and leave him in peace but it wasn't to be.

'By the way, it seems that you've got friends in high places because I've had special orders not to give you a hard time. I don't like special orders, but

I don't intend to lose my job over scum like you. So, I'll leave you alone, but if you step out of line and cause me any grief then you'll be having a little accident as well.'

Thomas wondered who it might have been who had given Motton his orders, but he doubted if Motton would follow them for long.

'I don't want any special favours,' Thomas replied. 'Just stick to the law and treat us all like human beings.'

Motton laughed out loud. 'There's only one law in here, and that's my law. You'll live a little longer if you keep that in mind.'

Motton left the cell, slamming the heavy door behind him. Any thoughts that Thomas had about killing Motton had gone, at least for now.

TEN

He was awakened on his first morning in prison by the rattle of keys and a vicious kick from Fletcher. 'Get up you lazy skunk, and strip those clothes off. We don't want you bringing your bugs in here, ain't fair on the other prisoners.'

Thomas paused after he'd removed the faded pants and check shirt that he'd been allowed to wear at Dalham Garrison.

'Get the rest off, no need to be shy. There aren't any saloon girls to laugh at your manhood.'

Thomas nearly tripped as he struggled to remove his long johns. He was thinking that they might be needed on the cold nights that came to these desert parts. When he finally stood as nature intended, Fletcher looked him up and down before ordering him outside, disappointed that he had no reason to mock anything he had just seen.

Roper and another guard named Burgess had arrived and both had a bucket of water in each hand. 'Jesus,' said Burgess, and then added, 'He's built like an ox.'

'Don't you mean, bull?' Roper laughed. 'Hey, Fletcher, he makes you look kind of puny.'

Fletcher scowled and then snapped, 'Stop the nattering and give the son of a bitch a good soaking.'

The first bucket of cold water took his breath away as it struck his chest. The second one was slowly poured over his head and when it was emptied on him he shook his head.

'He looks just like a puppy dog that's been in the river,' laughed Burgess.

Fletcher remained stony-faced and then ordered Thomas to push his clothes into the two buckets that still contained water. Once Fletcher was satisfied that the clothes were wet enough, he bellowed at Thomas, 'Get dressed again and then empty that shit bucket in the well across the yard and make sure you don't spill any. Then you can queue for some grub, if there's any left.'

Fletcher nodded to the other guards and all three left, leaving Thomas to struggle as he tried to wring out his wet clothes. He slipped more than once as he attempted to put his leg inside the wet pants, but eventually managed to dress, but he had left the long johns off.

The ablution bucket didn't have a handle so Thomas was forced to lift it with both hands and gingerly make his way out of the cell, holding his breath for as long as he could. He could see out of the corner of his eye that most of the cells had their doors open, and he discovered later that they were rarely locked.

He heard a muffled groaning sound coming from one cell, but kept his concentration and finally reached the outside of the block. He paused to steady himself for the short trip across the yard and squinted as the morning sun caught him full in the face. A glance to his left revealed the queue of about twenty men near what must be the grub table. Another group were sitting on the ground eating their morning ration of food which was hardly enough for a baby, let alone a full grown man.

Someone in the queue shouted out, 'Watch you don't drop it, Marshal.' Most of the other prisoners ignored him, but not the two men who were sitting close together, but apart from the others.

'Jesus, he sure looks old,' said Len Cooper. 'He'll die in here even without a helping hand from us. Perhaps we should just forget about him.'

Kyle Smith lifted his free hand to his face and stroked his fingers across the deep bullet crease in his cheek. 'No chance! We've got unfinished business with Thomas and don't you start making excuses. I ain't afraid of him even if he is a big evil bastard. There'll be two of us, and remember we'll have that knife of yours to cut him up real bad.'

Cooper was twenty-five years old and his baby face bore none of the scars of his boyhood friend Kyle Smith, but neither of them weighed more than 120 pounds. Their complexions were pale beneath their tanned faces, cheeks hollow, and their eyes were almost dead. Thomas saw them later but didn't recognize them as the men he had helped capture six years ago.

Smith and Cooper had only escaped a hanging for killing a storekeeper and his wife because they had agreed to take part in some medical experiments. Their present physical condition was the result of their stay at Yukron and nothing to do with the experiments.

Cooper had been pondering what his friend had said and laughed nervously. 'I ain't afraid of him. It's just that we could get out of here one day, but we won't if we stick the marshal with my blade. That's all I'm saying.'

Smith spat on the ground and snarled, 'No one's going to grieve if the marshal gets what's coming to him, least of all Motton, because he hates his guts. He made that clear when he told us Thomas was being sent here. It's best that we do it as soon as possible before the bastard settles in, and makes friends with some of the others or one of the guards looks after him. We'll do him tonight after grub time when we go back to the cells. Best stay out of his way until then if we can.'

'What do think happened to his eye, Kyle? He had two when we last saw him.'

'Who knows? I'm just glad whoever it was that skewered his eye out didn't finish him off. I couldn't believe our luck when I heard that he was coming here.'

'Why don't we just cut his eye out?' Cooper suggested, 'Then we could have a bit of fun teasing him as he stumbles about the place. That might give us more pleasure than just killing him.'

Smith finished licking the metal plate that had

contained a small handful of beans to go with a thin slice of stale bread as he thought about his friend's suggestion. Smith slowly stroked the scar on his face again. 'I like it, Len. That's one hell of good idea. We can always kill him after we get bored with teasing him. Yeah, that's what we'll do. We'll cut his frigging eye out.'

Cooper started sniggering at the thought of what he was about to say. 'I'm always hungry, Kyle, and a feller told me once that in some parts of the world they eat pigs' eyes. Well, Thomas is a pig.'

Smith wasn't even smiling as he was thinking that his friend had just come up with his second good idea. He would decide later whether they shared it, or tossed a coin to decide who got to eat the pig's eye.

By the time Thomas had made his way back to his cell with the empty bucket, Smith and Cooper had shuffled their way over to the main exercise area with the stooped gait of two very old men.

'Aren't you going to wait for some extras?' one of the prisoners had shouted after the pair. Everyone knew that there were no extras at Yukron, apart from when the occasional rat was caught or scraps of food were thrown to the ground at the end of meal time.

When Thomas finally got to the grub table the guard scraped the sides of the large pan that had been full ten minutes earlier. The dregs of the pan produced no more than a couple of mouthfuls, but the guard took pity as he watched Thomas staring at his plate, and gave him three thin slices of bread.

'Lesson number one, Marshal, is to make sure that you're never last in the queue,' was the grub man's advice.

Thomas walked from the table with his food and scanned the faces of those sitting with their empty plates. Some of them stared down as though wishing that the plate would suddenly be filled by magic. What struck him was how similar the prisoners looked, and then he remembered that skeletons usually did. One man who looked to be the oldest of the bunch gestured towards Thomas, inviting him to sit down.

'You don't remember me do you, Marshal?' the man with the grey, wispy hair asked. Thomas looked into the frail face of the enquirer, but failed to recognize him.

'I'm sorry, old-timer, but a lot of men have passed my way and I ain't very good at remembering faces, unless it belongs to a horse or perhaps a fine-looking woman.'

'Old-timer!' he chuckled. 'The name's Billy Lucas and I reckon I'm a good ten years younger than you are, but this place makes us all old before our time. Maybe this time next year we'll both be old-timers, but I hope not.'

'Billy Lucas, I remember now. You're from Caitlin County. I didn't mean any offence about you being an old-timer. I feel like one myself, what with my gammy leg.'

'No offence taken, Marshal, and there's nothing old-timer about you. Perhaps you'd like to take a walk around the exercise yard later and I'll explain some of the routine that we have here. If you want to keep in shape then you'll have to exercise because they don't give us any work to do. Then again, we wouldn't have the energy for work. We were given extra rations while we helped build the railway, but it didn't stop some prisoners from dying. Now Motton just hopes that we'll die from starvation, snake bites or do the job ourselves.'

Thomas insisted that Lucas take one of the slices of bread. 'I've been well fed for these past months, and like an old camel I've got plenty in reserve for now.'

As Thomas watched Lucas savour every nibble of the bread, he was thinking that Lucas's own ma wouldn't recognize the man who, just over eight years ago, had found his wife in bed with his best friend. Lucas had never been a violent man, but it hadn't stopped him from firing his rifle into the groin of his wife's lover when he had tried to escape. The judge had called it attempted murder, but Lucas had just wanted to make sure that his friend's womanizing days would be over, and he'd succeeded.

As they walked near the perimeter fence, Lucas explained the simple routine which meant sleeping and waiting for the next meal or funeral to take place.

The prison could cater for a maximum of sixty-five prisoners and Lucas was the longest serving one since Bowler, the previous occupant of Thomas's cell had died. Lucas had just finished talking about Bowler when they reached a small group of prisoners and someone shouted 'Snake'. The others repeated the cry and hastily backed away from the fence. Thomas instinctively followed the group and was startled by the crack of rifle fire from the watch-tower close to where they stood. Some of the prisoners cheered as the black and red snake fell from the fence on to the ground.

'I should have mentioned that happens on most days,' Lucas explained, 'but it's not just the snakes that you have to be careful of. I was just mentioning Bowler. Well, Bowler was accidentally shot dead by a guard who was aiming for a snake. He was daydreaming near the fence on his own and might have been thinking of going home. The poor guy was only a week away from being released.'

The evening grub was at least more substantial than the breakfast, or the faded piece of fruit they'd had at midday. The small piece of meat tasted like beef, but there were strong claims that the animal that it came from must have been used to carrying a saddle on its back. One of the prisoners, who had managed to keep his sense of humour, suggested that at least it was more tender than his wife's ma.

Lucas was keen for another chin-wag after the supper, but Thomas told him that he wanted to write a letter before it got too dark, and he headed back to his cell. It had only been an excuse, because likeable as though Lucas was, Thomas didn't want to get too close to him or anyone else at Yukron.

Lucas had told him that the guards were fairly lax about the time for locking up and most times didn't bother so Thomas was surprised when he heard footsteps approaching his cell as he lay on his bed.

'Howdy, Marshal, we thought we would come and sort of get reacquainted,' said Smith.

Thomas thought to himself 'Here we go again'. He didn't have a clue who the two men were, but sensed that they were not going to be as friendly as Billy Lucas.

'I'm Kyle Smith and this is Len Cooper. Remember us, Marshal?'

Thomas could remember their names even though he hadn't recognized their faces. He didn't know how they had managed to escape a hanging, but he knew that they hadn't come to welcome him. Smith had revenge written all over his miserable features, but it was Cooper who was holding the long-bladed knife. Thomas could sense that Cooper didn't have the stomach for whatever they planned, when he handed the knife to Smith as though he had just burnt his fingers on it.

'Here, you do him, Kyle. Cut out that scary-looking eye.'

Smith was taken by surprise, but he didn't have his friend's squeamishness.

'Right, hold the bastard down while I give him a matching pair.'

Thomas was struggling to get to his feet when Cooper dropped on top of him and Smith kneeled down trying to get a clear strike with the knife. Thomas growled like a wounded bear as he grabbed Cooper's shirt with both hands and hurled him sideways into Smith, causing the two men to become entangled and winded. Thomas scrambled to his knees and he grabbed the two men by their hair and slammed their heads together with a sickening thud. For a moment he thought that Cooper was dead, but he was soon groaning in unison with Smith. Thomas picked up the knife having already decided what he was going to use it for.

Motton was tucking his way through a giant plate of prime beef and sweet potatoes when one of the guards brought Thomas into his quarters. Motton hadn't been using a knife and he picked up the whiskey bottle with greasy fingers, took a long swig from it and belched before he spoke. 'This had better be important. I don't like being disturbed when I'm having my grub.'

The guard explained nervously, 'The marshal here reckons that your life's in danger, Mr Motton.'

'What are you talking about,' Motton growled in angry disbelief. 'Is this some kind of joke?'

'It's no joke,' replied Thomas, without waiting for the guard to speak. 'I'm going to take something from my pocket and put them on the table and then I'll explain.'

Motton was flushed with effects of the whiskey and still puzzled as to what this was all about, but he was alert enough to move his hand towards his pistol that was on the table.

'Jesus Christ, have you had an accident?' Motton asked, and then took another swig of whiskey as he stared at the two bloodied fingers that Thomas had dropped on to the table.

'They're not mine,' replied Thomas, showing

Motton that he had a full set of fingers on both hands.

'What the shit's going on here? Whose fingers are they?' Motton asked.

Thomas shrugged his shoulders. 'The truth is I don't really know for sure. They could belong to Len Cooper or they could belong to Kyle Smith. On the other hand, one might belong to Smith and the other to Cooper.'

'And what's all this got to do with my life being in danger?' Motton asked, but now more interested in his own welfare.

'Smith and Cooper came to my cell armed with a long-bladed knife intent on killing me, and they said that you would be next. I thought you ought to know.'

Motton staggered slightly as he got to his feet and picked up his gun from the table. 'Where's the knife, and the two lumps of shit who have been doing all this threatening?'

'They're in my cell. There was a bit of a scuffle and they got cut up a bit. You know yourself just how easy accidents can happen.'

'Right, let's go and sort this out,' ordered Motton, ignoring Thomas's jibe as he strode out of the room brandishing the gun.

Motton was still muttering to himself when they reached Thomas's cell door and heard the screams from Cooper, who had discovered that the middle three fingers of both hands had been hacked off.

Motton sobered up a little when he saw the array of fingers on the floor of the cell and he gasped when he rolled over the unconscious Smith and saw that as well as six fingers being missing, so was one of his eyes. The other guard turned away and puked just outside the cell door.

Motton shook his head at the carnage and then asked Thomas where the knife was. Having secured the knife that Thomas had hidden under the mattress, Motton barked at the guard to pull himself together and go and get Morris who was the nearest thing that the prison had to a medical man, not that he could do much to help these wretches. Motton was already thinking that what he had in mind for Smith and Cooper meant it would be a waste of effort trying to patch them up, but it would give Morris something to do.

Before Motton left he turned to Thomas. 'You're an evil son of a bitch, but I guess I owe you one. When Morris gets here tell him to make sure that those fingers are fed to the prison pigs, unless you want them for yourself.' Motton was still laughing when he left the cell block but he was already thinking that perhaps it would be better to keep out of Thomas's way, at least until he lost some of his strength.

It was some time after Morris had left and Cooper and Smith had been taken back to their cells when Thomas heard the screams that told him that Smith had regained consciousness. It appeared that Smith had discovered that he would only have one eye to rub from now on and a limited choice of fingers to do it with. Thomas knew how it felt to lose an eye, but there was no sympathy or feeling of regret for what he had done to Smith and Cooper. He had seized the opportunity to post a message to the other prisoners who carried a grudge against him. He knew how the minds of criminals and bullies worked. The disfigurement of Cooper and Smith would serve as a reminder to others to be wary of tackling him. There would always be that nagging doubt that he would get the better of his attackers and make them suffer, just like Cooper and Smith had.

The day after the incident with Cooper and Smith, Lucas identified some men who might come after Thomas, but none did. Some went out of their way to be friendly towards him while others avoided him.

It was nearly a week before Cooper and Smith ventured out and they made a sorry sight with both their hands heavily bandaged. Smith had a makeshift patch covering the hole where his right eye used to be. Later that night, Motton sent for them and he appeared sympathetic to what had happened to them.

'Sit down, boys, and have a drink,' Motton invited them and then watched them cup their glass of whiskey with their crippled hands.

'What happened to you both was a terrible, terrible thing, and it's been bothering me. So, I've decided to let you get your own back on Thomas.'

The two men faced each other, wondering what Motton had in mind. Smith's thirst for revenge was rekindled at the thought of what he might be able to do with Motton's help. But they were kept waiting while Motton took several gulps of whiskey before he continued. 'I'm going to give you your freedom, which is something that Thomas will never get.'

The recent torment left their faces as the news sank in, even though Smith was slightly disappointed, but the anguish returned when Motton added, 'I'm going to let you escape. What do think about that?'

Neither man was keen to answer. Motton was thinking that perhaps these two were not so stupid after all.

'But yours will be an escape with a difference, because nobody will be coming after you. I'll file a report that you died from natural causes. You can choose different names and start a new life. Of course you won't be able to return home, but it's a big world out there. Now I've had two saddle-bags of food made up. The train won't be moving for another week, so you can follow the railway track until you reach the station where you'll find a couple of horses in the stable. Just keep riding east and you'll be free men.'

Motton was surprised that neither man had shown any enthusiasm for a chance of freedom until Cooper asked, 'What about the snakes, Mr Motton?'

'Ah, the snakes.' Motton smiled before he explained. 'Now that you're leaving I can tell you that the stories about the snakes are exaggerated. I have one of the guards bring a snake close to the fence each morning so that the prisoners are kept frightened. Most of the snakes out there are harmless and the good news is that at the moment the snakes are in hibernation so you can walk across the plains without any fear.'

Smith and Cooper smiled, feeling reassured, and Motton was soon strapping the food bags on to their backs and escorting them to the prison gate and wishing them a safe trip.

The following morning, Motton was at the prison gate and shaking his head in dismay when the bodies of Cooper and Smith were carried in.

'When are the prisoners going to learn that escape is impossible with those snakes out there? I don't know who tried to help these men escape, but whoever it was, sent them to a certain death.'

Motton made a similar speech at the funeral of the men the following day and it brought a wry smile to Thomas's face.

Thomas had served just over a year when Billy Lucas was told that he was being released, and Thomas was pleased for the man who had become a friend.

When Lucas visited Thomas's cell just before he was going to catch the train out of Yukron, he asked Thomas a question that had been bothering him. 'Marshal, those names on your wall, Cropper and Linford? Are they important to you?'

'It's a very long story, Billy, but yes, they are important to me and they become more so with each passing day. I hope that one day they may help me clear my name, but time isn't on my side. I'll soon be an old-timer just like you, my friend.' Lucas smiled, remembering how Thomas had described him at their first meeting in prison. Before Lucas left the cell, he asked Thomas if there was anything he could do for him on the outside, and he was taken back by the request when Thomas handed him a twenty-dollar bill and asked, 'Try and locate a couple of books on poisonous snakes and send them to me. If you can't find any, then have a drink on me, Billy.'

Billy Lucas was dead within three months of leaving prison. The doctor had declared that Billy had died from natural causes, but being old before his time was the real reason. A month before he died, Billy had managed to buy two books on snakes and sent them to his friend Marshal Thomas. Luckily they arrived when Motton was on vacation and they were given to him. The books helped Thomas in more ways than he had hoped for, and he had started collecting dead snakes to use as food. He'd offered to share the snake meat with those inmates that he could trust, but despite their hunger they wouldn't eat the meat for fear of being poisoned.

ELEVEN

Thomas was nearly halfway through his second year at Yukron, when Motton began persecuting him, perhaps thinking that his protector in high places had lost interest or moved on.

Thomas was in the 'sweat box' for the sixth time in a month. The latest punishment was for not emptying his ablutions bucket, but it was widely known that the guards had used it after he had emptied it. Like on the other occasions, the trumped-up charge was the work of Motton. The box was barely big enough for him to squeeze into and was positioned outside where it would receive the full heat of the midday sun.

It was late afternoon on day four of his punishment when the two guards dragged him across the yard and dumped him in his cell. Some of the prisoners had started making bets that he wouldn't survive another visit to the sweat box, but Thomas had already decided that it was time for him to try and escape.

Once the guards had left his cell, Thomas drank

most of the water that had been left in a bottle nearby and then he eased himself off his mattress and crawled on his knees to the corner of his cell. He struggled to drag the ablutions bucket away from its usual position and started scraping away at the dirt. By the time he had retrieved the buried slivers of flint that he had rubbed down on the rocks, his fingers were bleeding. He had been using the longest of the three slivers to skin the small snakes that he'd found in the yard. They had either been left after being shot by one of the guards or abandoned by a mongoose.

He removed the dead snake that another prisoner had placed under his mattress while he had been in the sweat box and carefully dissected it until he reached the small pouch that held the serum. The next part of the operation required a steady hand while he made a small cut on his forearm and then dipped the sliver into the serum before mixing it into the blood of the open wound. As on previous occasions he had only just buried the slivers and repositioned the bucket when he felt the nausea coming on.

Within a couple of hours he was certain that he was closer to dying than he had ever been before. During the moments when he wasn't hallucinating he realized it had been a mistake to try and build up some immunity to snake venom to help him survive if he should get bitten after he had escaped.

The following morning he was drenched in sweat, but at least he was feeling better and vowing that if he survived he would forget his mad idea and take his chances without risking any more exposure to self-induced serum. His attempts to get off the mattress failed due to weakness and he abandoned the idea when he heard voices outside.

'I'm betting he's dead,' said Morris, the medical man.

'I ain't ever seen a corpse before,' replied Dawkins, who was a newly arrived guard, and the youngest recruit to the prison at the age of twenty-two.

'He looks dead, but he ain't,' said Morris. 'Best not to touch him or get too close in case he's got some sort of cotagsusis disease or whatever they call it.'

'What's that stink?' asked Dawkins, 'Is that what they call the smell of death?'

'I can't smell anything,' replied Morris, whose nostrils had become used to the foul smells around the prison. 'Anyway, leave him some water, and let's get out of here and tell Motton that he's still hanging on, but it won't be for long.'

'One of the guards reckoned that the old marshal must have been bitten by a snake, and that he was a goner for sure.'

Morris laughed. 'If he dies of a snake bite then he'll be the first prisoner here whoever did, and all the guards should know that by now.'

Dawkins looked puzzled. 'But I thought lots of the prisoners had died from snake bites.'

Morris shook his head, 'Most of the snakes out there are harmless except those in the hills, and unless you're unlucky they'll only make you feel a bit sick. All that bullshit about killer snakes was Motton's idea.'

'So how did those prisoners die?' Dawkins asked.

'From snake bites of course,' replied Morris with a smile. Dawkins wasn't the brightest individual and his brain was beginning to hurt, so he didn't ask any more questions and followed Morris out of the cell. Morris was eager to report Thomas's condition to Motton who had been getting increasingly angry about Thomas's physical condition being so good. Motton had threatened to beat anyone senseless if he found out that they had been giving Thomas extra food.

Thomas had heard everything Morris had said and it meant that he had risked his life for no good purpose. It also meant that most of the poor souls in the graveyard, including Smith and Cooper, had probably died from a bullet or a knife, and not from snake venom.

Within a few days, Thomas was well enough to venture out into the yard. The yellowness had left his skin and, although he was still weak, he was looking like his old self. The sight of Thomas brought a scowl from Motton as he passed through the yard, but he was out of sight when the guard on grub duty gave Thomas a few extra beans, and said, 'You can have those for all the meals you've missed, Marshal. You must be some sort of miracle man surviving that snake bite, or perhaps it was food poisoning.' The fat guard snorted as he tried to hold back laughing at his own joke, and then added, 'Anyway, you'll all be in line for a treat tomorrow. We're expecting a visit from some big wheel from Washington. He's arriving with a team of inspectors, so there'll be extra rations.'

Thomas spent the rest of the day outside taking in the fresh air and when he returned to his cell he slept, until he was shaken awake by Fletcher's boot.

'Motton wants to see you in his quarters. He said for you to bring any belongings that you want to keep. It looks as though you'll be on the move, and good riddance to you.'

Fletcher had disappeared before Thomas had fully shaken the drowsiness away, and even though he was suspicious of Motton he didn't have much option but to gather his things together. He ripped a strip off the blanket and wrapped it around the longest sliver of flint, placed it in his pocket and put the rest of his belongings in the small bag that Billy Lucas had left him.

Motton welcomed Thomas into his quarters like a long lost friend.

'Sit down, Marshal. I'm glad to see that you've recovered from your sickness. I'm afraid that some of the guards have been a bit heavy on you lately, because they might have misunderstood my instructions regarding your discipline. I suppose I didn't want to give the impression that you were being let off lightly because of you being a lawman. That's why I told them to lean on you, but they were a bit overzealous. Anyway, by my reckoning you've served enough time. I daresay you had a good reason for killing that general and he probably deserved it. So, by way of making amends for your rough treatment, I'm going to let you escape tonight and we won't be coming after you. I'll make sure that the records will show that you died in prison, so you just need to get yourself to Mexico and you can enjoy a life of freedom. I'm sure you'll be more than capable of surviving a few miles across the desert and then it should be easy after that. What do think?'

'I think you're trying to bullshit me, Motton,' Thomas replied.

Motton smiled back at Thomas. 'I thought you might show some gratitude, Marshal, but if you want to stay in prison then you can.'

'I'll take your offer but let's not play games. You don't expect me to survive, but I tell you that if I do, then I'll come after you one day, and that's a promise.'

'Sure you will, Marshal, but 1 don't expect I'll be seeing you again. Miracles don't happen in real life, but you hold on to your dreams.'

Motton beckoned to the guard who had stood near the door, and ordered him to escort the marshal to the main gate.

'Goodbye, Marshal,' Motton shouted after him. 'I've got to admit that you really have got balls after all.'

Thomas turned and glowered at Motton, wishing that he could have just five minutes with him on equal terms, but he would settle for his hope that Motton would face a hanging one day.

As Motton watched Thomas limp though the main gate he smiled with satisfaction, feeling that he had pulled off another master stroke. At sun-up tomorrow his men could finish Thomas off and he would be buried before the inspector arrived, preventing the lippy marshal complaining to any of the officials in the inspection party. He could have just had him killed inside the prison, but there was no fun in that. What he'd planned for him was much better.

The head guard was standing at the gate an hour after sun-up the following day when he saw the four guards ride back into camp with a body strapped to the horse that was being led by the guard at the rear. The broad smile disappeared when the group drew closer and he could see that it wasn't Thomas's body.

Motton was about to bawl out his deputy, Clay Johnson, for bringing back the body of the drifter who had probably died of thirst, but he was thinking that it might just rescue the situation. He ordered Johnson to go back out and search for Thomas on his own. The other guards were told to take the body to the makeshift morgue and prepare him to be buried later that day. Motton intended to preside over the burial of Marshal Thomas and his records would show that Thomas died from a snake bite after his escape.

Motton's last instruction to Johnson as he rode off on his solo search was, 'Find the bastard and kill him, but don't bring his body back.'

Johnson wasn't happy about going after the marshal on his own. He was about to tell Motton that he would need some help, but Motton was in a foul mood and Johnson decided it would be better to follow his instructions.

The deputy head guard reminded himself that the marshal was no fool and he might have avoided using the obvious escape route, expecting to be followed. And in any case they had already looked for him along the track. So, Johnson swung his mount in the opposite direction, and although he didn't have Motton's appetite for killing, he would finish off Thomas if he found him. Johnson had already decided that he would tell Motton that he'd killed Thomas even if his search drew a blank, and save himself from getting an ear bashing or worse.

Johnson had been searching for over an hour, and was beginning to suffer in the heat, when he steered his mount back towards the prison. As far as he was concerned, Thomas was officially dead.

When he reached the rocks close to the prison, he pulled on the reins to slow his mount down and then started looking out for snakes again. Johnson didn't trust Motton's assurance that the snakes were not deadly. But it wasn't a snake that caught his attention. 'Holy Jesus,' Johnson cried out, after he had spotted the figure come out from behind the rocks and stagger down the slope towards him, waving his arms. Johnson wondered what had happened to Thomas because he'd never seen blood streaming from beneath his eye patch before. The first shot that Johnson fired missed its target, but the second struck the face and the third buried itself into the chest. When he got closer to the body he fired a shot into the back of the head to avoid having to check whether the previous shots had done the job. Even Thomas couldn't have survived three bullets, including the one that had splattered his brains. Johnson had decided a long time ago that there was something not quite normal about Thomas. If Thomas had been normal, he would have been dead before now.

He wanted to take Thomas back to the prison as a trophy, but remembered Motton's orders, and opted to find a suitable place to leave the body, but it would have to be somewhere safe. Johnson was a God-fearing man and didn't think it was right that human beings should have the flesh picked from their bones by a creature, especially the vultures that often circled the valley. So he eased his conscience by dragging the body from where it lay, back towards the rocks, deliberately avoiding looking at what he imagined would be a gruesome sight.

While he was gathering suitable rocks to cover the body, he discovered a small ravine that would make an ideal hiding place, if he could manage to drag the body to it. By the time he had pulled the body up to the edge of the ravine he was in a state of collapse and needed to pause before he pushed it down. He worried that the body might become wedged in the narrow gap, but it landed with a thud ten feet below. The maggots would have a meal soon enough, but that was nature's way; at least the body would be out of the reach of vultures and other scavengers. As he made his way back to his horse he was pleased that his efforts had been worthwhile when he spotted a vulture circling above.

Johnson rode back to the prison at a gallop, forgetting about any danger from snakes, in his eagerness to report to Motton and tell him the good news.

When Johnson attended Thomas's fake funeral later, his thoughts kept drifting back to the ravine and the sight of blood streaming from the eye patch as Thomas had run towards him. It was a vision that would haunt Clay Johnson for a long time and make him consider going back to try and haul the body from the ravine and give it a proper burial.

TWELVE

Rose Cropper stared into the small cracked mirror after she had applied the powder to the dark rings below her eyes. It was only mid-afternoon but she had already consumed several glasses of whiskey to ease her depression. It had been over a week since she had been paid for her services. Luckily he hadn't noticed that she'd fallen asleep while she lay beneath him, because the last time that had happened she had been left with a missing front tooth and that hadn't helped business. At thirty-two she was the oldest of the girls who operated in Mira's Saloon, and by far the ugliest. The blonde hair was her best feature, but most drunken cowboys never looked beyond her ample breasts. Some declared that they were a sight to behold.

She still dreamed how life might have been if her husband Norman and the Carter brothers hadn't bungled the kidnap. She and Norman would have been living in a fine city house with a garden for little Belle to play in, instead of her being cooped up in this tiny house just off Palmerston Town's

Main Street. When Norman escaped she'd hoped that they would still be able to settle somewhere better than this. The letter that had arrived a month after the escape had been full of promises, and she had believed him. At least the money that he sent with every letter over the following six months had helped her manage. He couldn't tell her where he was living, but promised that they would all be reunited and soon. Then the letters had suddenly stopped. She didn't know whether he was dead, or had met someone else. Her Norman wasn't the sort of man who could do without a woman for too long, no more than could she do without a man. She hadn't decided to sell her body just for the money. She had needs that had to be satisfied as well.

She had finished applying the thick rouge and getting ready to walk to the saloon, when she was startled by the loud banging on the front door. She hoped it was a private client and he would want to stay for the night. Madame Mira would bar her from the saloon if she found out, but it meant extra money for Rose because she didn't have to pay for the use of the room at the saloon. She hurriedly smoothed the bed sheets and was about to clear the dirty dishes from the table when the banging started again.

'Easy, tiger,' she said, forgetting about the mess on the table as she squirted some cheap perfume into the air, pulled down the top of her dress to reveal more flesh and then finally opened the door.

'You're eager, honey,' said Rose, before she had determined if the caller was a former client. She usually remembered the good-looking ones, but on closer inspection she wouldn't have forgotten this one easily, because he only had one eye. In the short time that she had been selling her body she had encountered the occasional customer who didn't have a full set of body parts and she was tired of the crude comment: 'Don't worry, honey, I've still got the most important bit.'

'I'm open for business, mister, if that's why you're here,' Rose announced, looking him up and down. 'Did someone recommend me?'

Thomas was thinking that he'd made a mistake because he had been told that Rose Cropper was a respectable lady, but he wasn't the sort to be impolite to a woman, not even a common whore like this one.

'I was hoping to see Mrs Cropper; I'm a friend of her husband,' Thomas lied.

Sadness appeared on her face for a moment. 'I haven't been called that in a while, honey. I'm Rose Cropper.' She ushered Thomas in and directed him to a seat near the bed which she then flopped on to as she tried to lower herself. He explained that he wasn't exactly a friend, but he was ready to offer money in return for information, and was disappointed to discover that she hadn't heard from her husband in a long time.

'It would help if you could just tell me where he was when he last contacted you. I promise you that I don't intend your husband any harm. As it happens, I'm sort of beholden to him.'

Rose was beginning to warm to the man who still

hadn't introduced himself. On closer inspection he wasn't that old. He looked attractive, in an odd sort of manly way. There was something strong about him, and she wondered how long it had been since he'd slept with a woman. She was hoping that he might provide some business after all, and if not, she might even offer it for free. She was lost in her thoughts when Thomas asked her again about the whereabouts of her husband.

'Sorry, I was just having some pleasant thoughts,' she replied, and then smiled at Thomas in a way that disturbed him, even though he was well used to being propositioned. 'I should have his last letter somewhere, and I could let you have that, if you paid me for it.'

'I'll give you ten dollars even if it's no use to me, but it might be better if you read it first, just in case there's anything personal in it.'

It took a few minutes of rummaging in a cupboard before the letter was found and she read through it in silence. She wiped the tears away, smudging the rouge on her face.

'There are a few bits of what you might call personal. My Norman is a red-blooded man and he tells me how he misses our love-making. Well, he calls it something different, but I'm sure you know what I mean. The fact is I'm missing him as well, especially at night. I've tried to stay pretty hoping that he would come back, but I'm afraid I have needs. I have so much love to offer that's going to waste. That's why I hang out at Mira's Saloon.'

She paused, hoping that Thomas would make

115

some comment, perhaps even give her a compliment, but when he didn't, she read out the piece that might be of some interest to him. 'Norman says here, that by the time I get this letter the railroad will have arrived where he is, and that'll be good for business so it won't be long before he sends for me and little Belle.'

Rose dabbed her eyes with a small flower-patterned handkerchief, but this time Thomas couldn't see any signs of a tear. When she took the ten-dollar bill, she told him that it would go towards her rail fare so that she could join her little girl who was staying with her folks back East.

Cropper's letter hadn't been dated and Rose didn't seem very convincing when she said that it arrived about six months ago or maybe it was longer, or it might have been less. As she pushed the money down her cleavage she gave Thomas another coy look and then declared, 'I've just realized who you are. You're that marshal who stopped the kidnapping.' Then she acted in mock anger. 'I ought to hate you for spoiling my plans.' Her eyelashes fluttered again when she added, 'But I don't. My Belle thought you were a nice man, and so do I. I'm right, I know I am. You're the man with the patch.'

Thomas didn't think it wise to confide in a woman like Rose and said, 'I don't wear a patch, and I think it's best that you don't know too much about me, except that my name's Ned.'

She didn't push him any further, but insisted that he had some coffee before he left and it gave him a chance to mull over a proposition he intended to put to her, which would mean that he would be staying the night.

Thomas had spent the past two months sleeping mostly under the stars with the occasional stay in some deserted cabin or barn. He had managed to buy food and supplies without venturing into the big towns where he would be in danger of being arrested. Now he had the chance of some comfort, at least for a while.

Rose Cropper accepted his proposition, but she seemed disappointed that he would be sleeping alone and he would have to resort to lies before she stopped flaunting herself at him. When she had headed off for 'work' telling him that she would be back in the morning, Thomas had turned the sheets over and settled into her bed.

It wasn't the first whore's bed that he'd slept in but it felt the most comfortable after sleeping rough and his stay at Yukron. Before he drifted off to sleep, his thoughts of the thin mattress on the cell floor at Yukron had him reliving the sequence of events that took place on the morning after Motton had allowed him to escape.

He had watched the comings and goings outside the prison gate from his vantage point up amongst the rocks, and he cursed when he saw the rider heading in his direction. With luck, his pursuer would keep to the trail and ride past him. If he didn't, then Thomas would be at his mercy because the fall he had taken during the night severely restricted his movement and his knee was hurting like hell. It had been a mistake to try and push on when the light was so poor, but he had never doubted that Motton would send someone after him. Thomas wanted to get as far away from the prison as possible, but he was no more than 500 yards away. If he could get through today and the knee improved, then he could start his journey to freedom tomorrow. At least he had food and water, or so he thought.

The rider didn't seem in any hurry, with his mount moving at no more than a gentle trot, and was within a few hundred yards when Thomas recognized the squat figure of Clay Johnson. The guard's preoccupation with the ground around him suggested that at the moment he was more interested in snakes than finding Thomas.

It seemed an age before Johnson passed by, and then galloped off, much to the relief of Thomas, but he still waited until his pursuer was some distance away before he carefully lowered himself to the ground and removed the water bottle from the bag. Whatever the liquid was that he spat against the rocks after his first swig from the bottle, it certainly wasn't water. He emptied the contents on to the ground and watched it soak into the parched sand. A quick foray inside the bag for food revealed a number of small stones, and rotten pieces of wood. Motton had planned that he die of thirst or starvation if he managed to evade being found while he was still alive.

At least his present location was sheltered from the sun and that was some consolation. He had been unlucky that Motton's offer of escape had been forced on him before he'd had the chance to prepare his own escape. At least he would have had taken some supplies, including water, although his escape route would have been just the same. His plan was to hold up this side of the prison and then eventually work his way back through the valley and leave the way he'd been brought in by Jewson and Symes. There was more danger of being picked up, but the alternative was a 200-mile trek across the desert in the direction of where Johnson was heading. The mountain ranges to the north and south might have been an option for someone younger, but not for him, even before he had damaged his knee. He'd never been comfortable with heights since he had trailed a wanted man into the mountains, and nearly slipped into a ravine. He had managed to pull himself to safety but it had cost him a ruptured arm muscle.

The pain from his injured knee had made sleeping difficult during the night and he had been dozing when he heard the snorting of a horse. He sat up instinctively, forgetting his injury, and gritted his teeth to stop crying with pain. Sound could travel far in these surroundings and he was hoping that Johnson was further away than the snort from the horse indicated. The second snort left him in no doubt that someone was just a matter of feet away. He was pulling the sliver of flint from his pocket when he heard the hiss. He had forgotten the name of the black and yellow snake whose raised head was staring at him. Thomas remained motionless but it didn't stop the snake from striking, and for a moment the pain in his knee was replaced by the one in his cheek where the fangs had struck. Thomas lurched forward to grab the snake and then cried out as he felt the searing pain in his knee. He was struggling to hold the wriggling snake, which was close to four feet long, when he saw the face of the rider. His pursuer was fumbling to get his pistol out of its holster, perhaps due to panic or being inexperienced at drawing a pistol while on horseback. It might have been the sight of the snake that Thomas had flung, or the sudden movement of Thomas that caused the horse to rear its front legs sending its rider crashing against the rocks. The cracking sound of the skull against the hard rock meant that the rider hadn't felt the pain from the snake bite to his neck for very long.

'Easy, boy, easy,' said Thomas, grateful that the animal hadn't galloped away. Its eyes were wide with fear and it had fidgety legs, but he soon had it under control.

Thomas had seen that same lifeless look and staring eyes more times than he would wish on any man. He was glad that it wasn't Johnson and it seemed as though Motton was on his way to the gates of Hell.

When Rose Cropper left her house three days after she had first opened her door to Thomas, she was dressed in a simple cream calico dress and a matching hat. The dress was loose fitting and helped hide the bump that seemed to be getting bigger by the day. Perhaps when the baby arrived she might have a better idea who the father might be from a long list, but she doubted it, because she couldn't remember what most of them looked like.

There were a few surprised faces when she walked down Main Street to catch the stagecoach that would take her the ten miles to Dalham City to start a train journey that would end with her being reunited with her daughter.

When she'd told her neighbours that her old uncle would be staying at her house for a while, some of them had given her a knowing look. She heard one of the women say in a lowered voice, 'The hussy.'

Ned had given her back some self-respect and she was grateful for that, as well as the money. She still wished that she could have repaid him in some way, and brought a bit of pleasure to his life as well as her own. She had known much older men than him who had surprised her with their performance beneath the sheets and she had been disappointed when he had turned down her offer of spending the night together, for free. Ned might have been the answer to her prayers. He appeared to have money and he was handsome in an odd way. She had gotten used to him looking at her with just one eye, but when he told her he had been badly wounded 'down below' that had put an end to any idea of her trying to snare him. They had danced around what he meant by 'down below' until Thomas had finally blurted out, 'I can't get it up. That's what it means. I'm like a bull that's been snipped.' Rose didn't know what to say except, 'You, poor man.' The proposition that Thomas had made to her, which she had gladly accepted, was that he would give some money for clothes and her train ticket so that she could join her daughter in return for the use of her house as a base.

Thomas had promised that he would send any news about her husband to the address that she'd left him, but she doubted if she would ever be reunited with her husband. He wouldn't take too kindly to the little bundle that she was carrying in her swollen belly, especially when it couldn't possibly be his.

Thomas waited until the time had passed when Rose should have been on the stagecoach, and then he ventured out to the local store. Palmerston Town was little more than an overgrown staging post and hardly warranted being called a town, but he was surprised that it had a sheriff, and the store was well stocked. He was thumbing through a book on the Union Pacific Railway when the storekeeper asked him if he had an interest in the subject.

'I was just wondering if the book would show any expansion to the rail system, but I expect it's a hard job to keep up with things changing so rapidly.'

Silas Pamment, the storekeeper, was a railroad enthusiast and was eager to share his knowledge with anyone who showed the slightest interest.

'Depends what sort of area you're talking about and whether you mean just in this state.'

The poser took Thomas by surprise, not knowing just how far Cropper might have fled, so he covered himself by saying, 'I'm interested in an area of about a hundred miles from here, so I guess that would cover here and a bit of Nevada. I have a special interest in any new stations that were introduced in the last six months or thereabouts.'

'Well, then, you're talking about a lot of expansion that would include maybe ten towns or more, mostly along the banks of the River Teako which runs into Nevada. I'm not sure about the specific time that you mentioned though.' Pamment paused and ruffled what little hair he had left. 'They were planning a stretch from Dalham up to Rutland County until they gave up trying to blast a way through the mountains.'

Thomas left the store with his supplies and a copy of the book on railways, not that he had any interest in damned trains, but he was still grateful that they weren't as reliable as a good horse after his experience travelling to Dalham and his meeting with Henry Tyler. That trip seemed a lifetime away now.

He trudged back to his temporary home, thinking that his search for Cropper would be like trying to find a needle in a haystack. He wasn't even certain how Cropper could help him, but he was at a loss as to what else he could do, except maybe to head for Mexico and forget the whole thing.

Later that night after finishing off the last of whiskey that was left in the house, Thomas had decided that finding Cropper was a lost cause. So tomorrow he would begin the long ride to Mexico. He was about to turn in and looking forward to a good night's sleep now that things were settled in his mind, when he heard the loud knock on the door. Thomas struggled out of the chair and smiled at the thought that if the caller was after Rose Cropper's services then he would soon be in for a shock.

The young man was shocked, but for a different reason, because the man who had opened the door was supposed to be dead, and he had even visited his grave.

Thomas was certain that he knew the man, but he couldn't put a name to the face or where he had met him.

'Marshal Thomas?' the caller enquired.

'Do I look like a marshal?' Thomas replied, as he struggled to identify the man. He was certain that it wasn't Cropper. Not unless he had disguised himself as an officer in the United States Army.

'Anyway, never mind who I am. Who are you, and what's your business here? If you come lusting after the woman, she don't live here any more.'

'Marshal, don't you recognize me? I'm Anderson. I defended you at your trial.'

'You ain't come to arrest me?' Thomas asked, and peered outside in case Anderson wasn't alone.

Anderson smiled, puzzled by what Thomas had said.

'Well, I wouldn't be here to arrest you, when I thought you were dead. I was told by the town sheriff that a man was staying here. We asked him to report anything suspicious that might involve Cropper. Incidentally, we have Cropper in custody, but it's all a bit of a secret.'

Now Thomas was puzzled as he invited Anderson to step inside. Judging by Anderson's comments about thinking he was dead, it looked as though someone had found Motton's body. Thomas had swapped clothes with Motton, and cut out his eye with the sliver of flint. He'd covered the gaping hole with his own patch and it appeared as though his plan must have fooled someone at the prison. But he would soon be left wondering what the hell had really happened after he had fled on Motton's horse leaving him against a rock.

'What made you think I was dead, or did you just assume that I didn't survive my escape?' Thomas asked, after the two men had sat down near the table.

'Well it's a long story, but I'll try and keep it short. About two months ago I was given an assignment to deliver a message to you at the prison. Even though I was no longer working in the legal branch . . . but I'll explain about that later. By coincidence, I travelled with the prison inspector's team. I went to inform you that you were to be given a special pardon as part of an amnesty given by the President prior to his resignation due to his failing health.'

Thomas shook his head in disbelief. 'You mean I was cleared of killing General Stanmore?'

'No, it wasn't quite like that, but it meant that you would be released from prison, if you agreed not to disclose any details of the kidnap and to have no contact with the Press.'

'So you must have arrived at the prison the day after I escaped, or, as it happens, was allowed to escape by Motton, the head guard.'

'I did,' Anderson confirmed. 'When we arrived, the place was in chaos. Motton had gone missing and we found out why later.'

Thomas interrupted Anderson, expecting that he was about to be told that Motton had been found dead. 'Yukron Valley isn't the place that anyone would want to go missing. I can vouch for that.'

'Well I suppose missing is the wrong word really. Motton fled before the inspector arrived, otherwise he would be in prison himself now, or, more likely, would have faced a hanging. You can imagine my horror when I was told that you had been found dead near the railway tracks, apparently the result of multiple snake bites. Instead of delivering you the good news I was taken to the grave where you had apparently been buried just a couple of hours earlier. Was it some sort of plan that you arranged with Motton to fake your death?'

Thomas offered Anderson some coffee, hoping it would give him time to gather his thoughts and decide how much to tell him. When the offer was declined, Thomas tried his best to come up with a convincing story.

'To tell you the truth, I'm not sure what to make of what you have just told me about your visit to Yukron, but I didn't make any deal with Motton, or anyone else at the prison.'

'Perhaps Motton was genuine in letting you go,' Anderson suggested, 'and they had a mock burial just to keep the records straight. Although, it all seems a bit complicated and from what I heard of the man, it didn't seem the sort of gesture that Motton would make. We may never know whether he got clear of the desert and is living on his ill-gotten gains.'

Thomas thoughts were back at the spot amongst the rocks where he had left Motton's body and he assumed that it was still there.

'So where does all of this leave me, son? Am I a free man, or a wanted man?'

Anderson puffed out his cheeks and sighed. 'That's an interesting question, Marshal. I would need to check with my superiors, but I don't see any reason why you can't still be given the pardon if you agree to the conditions I mentioned. Legally speaking, you are an escaped prisoner, but that can be sorted out. It wasn't as if you harmed anyone during your escape. I still think that there is a chance that we can prove your innocence.'

Thomas was thinking that he had only caused Motton to have his brains smashed against the rocks, and then cut his eye out.

Thomas shook his head, 'I can hardly believe that this is happening, but I don't see how you can hope to prove my innocence.'

'Marshal, there are still things you don't know about. I'd better explain a little about my own situation and then I'll bring you up to date. By the way, did you ever get the money that I sent for the sale of your stallion? You never replied to any of my letters so I assumed that you just wanted to be left alone?'

Thomas apologized for not replying, even though he had never received either money or letters from Anderson. It was likely that Motton had pocketed the money, and Thomas was feeling less guilty about using the proceeds of the money that he'd found in Motton's saddle-bags that had helped him since his escape and just helped Rose Cropper.

Anderson proceeded to tell him that after the trial he had become disillusioned at the prospect of a life in the legal branch and had transferred to a specialist unit which involved real soldiering, or at least the prospect of seeing some action. He had been assigned to a special investigation connected to the kidnapping and Stanmore's murder. He had always felt that Cropper had been allowed to escape, and still believed this was the case.

Thomas interrupted him. 'But you said he was in custody. Has he told you about his escape? I expect you must have guessed that's why I'm here. I was hoping that Cropper might be able to help me in some way to find out who killed the general. I didn't know how, but I suppose I was thinking that Cropper might have had an accomplice inside Dalham Garrison.'

'I don't think Cropper can throw any light on what you are suggesting. He hasn't told us anything useful so far, and insists that he wasn't allowed to escape.'

Thomas wasn't sure why Anderson could make such a confident statement about Cropper and he wondered how Rose would react to the news that her husband had been recaptured. When he mentioned about meeting Rose Cropper and his promise to let her know if he found out anything about her husband, he was surprised when Anderson said, 'I think it's best if you don't contact her about her husband until we know what's going to happen to him.'

'If that's what you want,' Thomas said, but there was something else still bothering him and he asked if any details had ever surfaced about his weapon being tampered with. He also mentioned that he would like to know who he had to thank for delivering him the warning note.

'It was Major Linford, who passed you the note,' said Anderson.

'Well, I'll be damned. I always suspected that it was him. I hope I'll get to thank him.'

'There are a few things you should know, Marshal, but they must remain confidential. Although Major Linford delivered the note, it was under General Stanmore's orders.'

'I don't understand. According to Linford, it was the general's idea to have my weapon taken off me and have it serviced.'

'General Stanmore must have felt guilty about having to agree with the Carters' demand to tamper with your pistol, and for not making you aware of the danger you were about to face.'

'I've been in the business a long time, son, and got to trust my instinct. What you say about Stanmore doesn't fit, but then again there had to be a reason for him being murdered and perhaps it was tied up with the kidnapping. I'd still like to thank Major Linford.'

Anderson sighed. 'The other thing that you

should know is that Major Linford was placed under arrest two days ago, and is being questioned about a number of things connected with the kidnapping.'

'Jesus,' Thomas gasped. 'All this is too much for a simple lawman like me to take in. You'll be telling me next that the major killed General Stanmore.'

'He is being questioned about that as well, because he was the last known person to see the general. You might recall from your trial that it was established that he stayed behind in the general's office when you and Captain Jameson left after the debriefing.'

Thomas had gone from wanting to thank Linford, to wishing that he would rot in hell if he had been responsible for him being sent to Yukron prison.

Anderson could see that Thomas was shocked by the news and decided it was time to leave. 'I would suggest that you keep your head down until you hear from me,' Anderson advised. 'I would hope to return in a couple of days after checking out the position as regards your pardon, but I'm sure there won't be any problems.'

After Anderson left, Thomas was wishing that there was more whiskey in the house because he knew that he wouldn't be able to sleep easily after what he'd been told. It grieved him that he might have misjudged Stanmore so badly and that he was beholden to him for his life. Anderson was a good man, but he was young and perhaps a little naive in believing that he could prove Thomas's innocence. Life wasn't that simple. If Cropper and Linford stayed dumb, then Thomas's position wouldn't change. By the time Thomas had drifted into a deep sleep he was thinking that he would settle for a pardon and retirement.

When Anderson returned to the Cropper house two days later, Thomas could tell that he was troubled about something. The young captain accepted a drink of whiskey from the replenished stocks that Thomas had bought and then he explained the results of his meetings with his commanding officer.

'I've managed to secure your pardon, but my CO, Colonel Clayton wants you to help us.'

Thomas didn't like the sound of this, and asked, 'Is this some sort of condition?'

'Not really, but he does think that you could help with the kidnapping investigation and wants you to go and see General Mosley to get his permission to billet at the garrison for a short while. Colonel Clayton hopes that this might somehow flush out those who were involved in the kidnapping if they feel the pressure from your presence. If you'd rather not get involved you will still get your pardon.'

Thomas couldn't see how what was being suggested could help, but didn't want to appear ungrateful, even though he would be putting himself in the firing line again. He'd always got on with General Mosley so he agreed to go along with the idea.

'Good! Now, I expect you'll want to get ready for your meeting with the general this afternoon.'

Thomas was taken aback that he would be going to the Dalham so soon. 'Don't you need to arrange things? I can't just barge in on the general.'

Anderson smiled. 'Everything's been arranged with General Mosley, but there are some things that he doesn't know, and mustn't find out, but I'll brief you on those later. I hope you don't mind me jumping the gun, but I knew that you'd want to help in any way you can.'

It was Thomas's turn to smile. 'I keep forgetting that you're a trained lawyer and they can never be trusted.'

THIRTEEN

As Thomas waited in the corridor outside General Mosley's office his thoughts were back at his trial. The general had appeared sympathetic to his plight even though he had been accused of killing a senior officer. Mosley had a reputation for being a straight talker and not a bullshitter, like some of his kind. Maybe in the next few minutes Thomas would find out if Mosley still believed that Thomas was guilty.

The general hadn't changed much apart from being a bit fuller in the body and his face appeared flushed.

'You're looking well, Thomas. Perhaps your ordeal wasn't so bad after all. But I'm sure it wasn't very pleasant. I must say that I was surprised to hear that you want to go along with this idea of staying at the garrison.'

'If there's any chance of proving my innocence then I'll take it, General.'

'I can understand that, Thomas, but you need to be careful. The army has changed from the one that we knew. All this cloak and dagger stuff. It all smacks of a hidden agenda and unnecessary secrecy. To be honest with you, I don't really trust this feller Anderson, or those he works for.'

The comment about Anderson took Thomas by surprise, but coming from someone like Mosley it had to be taken seriously. When Thomas didn't comment, Mosley continued, 'I don't suppose I should criticize a fellow officer, but I didn't join the army to be a diplomat, no more than you did all those years ago. I expect you have heard about Major Linford being arrested. It's an absolute disgrace, and I'll have something to say to this Colonel Clayton who appears to be running the show, if ever I get to meet him. Major Linford is a fine officer and I can't visit him to offer him my support. I don't care what happens to that blighter, Cropper, but Major Linford is a different matter. I don't even know where he is being held.'

Mosley's fury was complete when he thumped the oak desk with a clenched fist.

'Damn, I'm a senior officer, and I'm not kept in the picture about what's happening. It just isn't right. So you watch your back, Thomas, because you might be being used in a way that won't bring you any benefit. If you take my advice you'll ride out of here and settle for having your freedom. Even if these characters from the intelligence section are above board, they're still putting you at risk.'

Thomas reminded himself that he didn't really know much about Anderson, although he appeared genuine enough. It had seemed an odd coincidence him just turning up at the Cropper house like he had, claiming to have been tipped off by a local sheriff that Thomas had never seen.

Thomas was still mulling over what Mosley had said when the general gave him some more food for thought. 'Did Anderson tell you that he knew Cropper before he joined the army?'

'He's never mentioned it, but I don't suppose it matters. Does it?' Thomas asked.

'Maybe not,' replied Mosley. 'But in my view Cropper is as guilty as the Carter brothers and should meet the same fate. The man's a crook and Anderson knew him. I would have thought he would have at least said something to you. Anyway, you seem determined to see this thing through, so my admin officer will arrange for you to stay at Dalham Garrison for as long as you want. I am off to Washington in a few days and I'm not sure when I'll be back so there's a chance that I won't see you again. Good luck, Thomas, and remember what I said about being careful.'

Thomas was surprised by the abruptness in which Mosley ended their meeting, but the general was a busy man and must have felt that there was nothing more to be said. Thomas was about to reach for the door handle when Mosley called out, 'Thomas, there is something that you might be able to do for me while you are at the garrison.'

During his first night at the garrison as Thomas lay on his bed in the single barrack room, his mind was in turmoil as he tossed around the various things that Mosley had told him. Perhaps he should take

Mosley's advice and just leave. Eventually, he decided that in the morning he would tell Anderson that he had reconsidered his position and that he wanted to leave the garrison. This time tomorrow he would be on his way home. He wondered what sort of reception he would get when he returned to Statton Crossing and what condition his house would be in. He was woken by the raucous laughter from some soldiers in a nearby billet. Thomas was struggling to get back to sleep long after the soldiers had settled down, when he heard the sound near his door. He planned to give the soldiers the shock of their lives if they were intent on playing some stupid game, like tipping him out of his bed. If it wasn't a prankster then whoever it was turning the handle wasn't lost because they were trying their best not to awaken the occupant. He'd heard tales of saloon girls creeping into a soldier's bed and snuggling up to them, leaving the financial arrangements until later. Rose Cropper came to mind!

Just before the door was opened Thomas pretended to be asleep by making some gentle snoring sounds, but he had tensed his body ready to react, wishing that his pistol was within reach. His visitor paused when the floorboards gave a loud creak, but was soon creeping towards him again. Thomas saw the raised arm and rolled to his side, and crashed to the floor as he avoided the downward thrust of a knife blade which buried itself in the mattress where Thomas had been lying. His attacker pulled the knife free and dived on to the winded Thomas, but was thrown aside as Thomas recovered. He was accustomed to the dim light now and could clearly see the man's raised arm as he made another attempt to strike with the long-bladed knife. Thomas gripped the man's wrist, and forced it down at the same time as he rolled to the side, uncertain as to where the knife would finish up. The gasp from his attacker, followed by a groan, told him whose flesh the knife had penetrated.

The intruder had stopped groaning by the time that Thomas had risen to his feet and fumbled to light the lamp. The flickering light had reached full glow before Thomas recognized the intruder. The face had been immediately familiar to him but there was something different about it. The face was fuller than he'd remembered it, but there was no doubt who it was, or that he was dead.

Thomas was still breathing heavily from the exertion of the struggle when he reached for the large watch that was attached to the heavy chain. It was 2.15 in the morning and he needed to decide his next move. The guardroom would be manned and the sensible thing to do was to report the incident in case someone came to investigate what the disturbance was. It looked as though the flushing out plan had worked already, but Thomas expected that merry hell would break out when his attacker's identity was revealed.

The guardroom was no more than a few hundred yards away, and he was soon scaring the living daylights out of the lonely sentry who had been cat-napping.

'Jesus, what are you doing about at this time, Marshal?'

Thomas explained what had happened and Private Kirby let out another 'Jesus.' And then asked Thomas what he should do.

'You'd better shake one of the other guards awake and get him to report what has happened to the duty officer. I'll go back to my room and wait for him. I'm using a room in the block next to the cook-house. I'll leave my door open.'

It was mid-morning when an exhausted Thomas found himself recounting the events leading to the death of Captain Jameson once more. This time it was to General Mosley, and his mood was quite different to the previous day's meeting in the same location.

'If we were in a war situation, Marshal, I would be sending you home. I would have come to the conclusion that you are some kind of jinx, even a liability.'

Thomas resented being labelled in this way because he knew that Mosley wasn't trying to make a joke.

'Have you any idea why Captain Jameson would want to see you dead, Thomas? Did you two have any sort of history?'

Thomas wasn't sure what the general was getting at and asked him to explain. 'What do you mean by history, General?'

'I mean, did you two have any grievances, like you and General Stanmore had?' replied Mosley, clearly irritated by Thomas's question.

'I met him on the day of the kidnap, and we only shared a couple of dozen words, so there was hardly any time for what you call history.' Thomas's reply was delivered with an obvious anger which was detected by Mosley who softened his approach. 'This is a sorry business, Marshal, and I can see that it's not of your making. Perhaps the captain was planning to take revenge for what he believed you had done to General Stanmore.'

Thomas had calmed down when he replied, 'That theory has been put to me more than once this morning General, and I suppose it makes sense.'

'What does Captain Anderson have to say?' Mosley asked, as he fiddled with the small paper-knife on his desk.

Thomas told the general that he hadn't seen Anderson, and he didn't mention that he was curious himself to know what Anderson would make of it.

Mosley placed the paper-knife on the desk and straightened up in the leather chair, having come to a conclusion.

'I've decided that the best thing is for you to leave the garrison this morning, Marshal. I'll inform Anderson that I'm not prepared to continue with his *flushing out* experiment. It would be ludicrous to link Captain Jameson's attempt on your life to whatever Anderson is investigating. So, in everyone's interest, not least of all your own, I want you to check out of the barracks once you leave here, never to return, and that's an order.'

'That suits me, General. I was intending to leave anyway.'

Mosley seemed surprised. 'I think it would have been a wise decision, Marshal, even though from a selfish point of view it may have been useful having someone around who I can trust. You could have kept watch on what Anderson was up to. By the way, if you have any news about what we discussed yesterday, perhaps you will pass it on to my admin officer before you leave.'

When Thomas told him that he had found out what he wanted to know, the general smiled and said, 'Good man, Marshal. I'm glad you have remained loyal to me, and I won't forget it.'

Corporal Mickey Slater had been proud when he had been assigned to the special unit, thinking that it would involve doing something different to ordinary soldiering. Now he was spending his third night guarding a makeshift cell block in a rundown old farmhouse, and he wouldn't get to see another soul until his relief turned up at eight o'clock in the morning. Not even a pep talk from Captain Anderson had made him feel any better. It wasn't as if he was on army land, and he felt that he was doing something useful. The farmhouse wasn't fit for a prisoner let alone a soldier on guard duty.

Anderson had told him that what he was doing was vital to national security, and his spell of guard duty would soon be over. In the meantime, he wasn't to tell anyone about what he was doing or reveal the location of the house which was six miles from the garrison at Dalham.

Slater had polished his boots and cleaned his pistol before he settled into the rocking chair on the porch and lit up the small cigar. It was a clear night and he had a good view of the woods some fifty yards in front of the cabin. It seemed quiet tonight but he was certain that he'd seen some movement there last night. At least he could relax tonight and think about which of the saloon girls he would spend his pay on, but it wasn't an easy choice. He had finally settled on it being Anne Marie when he heard a rustling sound coming from the woods. It was probably just an animal foraging around, but Slater wasn't convinced. He took a final nervous puff on the cigar, flicked the stub to a spot close to the water trough, and then backed up until he reached the door.

He settled back in the chair facing the door and then placed his pistol on the table in front of him. He was thinking that perhaps he should have locked the door, but felt it wasn't the manly thing to do.

'Time for some grub,' he said to himself, as he reached into the saddle-bag and pulled out the chunky bread and pieces of dark yellow cheese. He should have saved some for the morning, but he was soon chopping through the last of the pieces.

The effect of the meal caused Slater to doze off, and the sound of footsteps on the boards of the porch didn't register at first. He thought they were part of dream, but the bang on the door soon had him fumbling for his pistol as he struggled to his feet. He was about to challenge what he thought was an intruder, but stuttered with embarrassment when he recognized who it was.

'Sorry, sir, I thought it was an, an . . .' Slater didn't finish his sentence as he replaced his pistol in its holster. 'I wasn't expecting any visitors tonight.'

'You should have been informed, Soldier, but not to worry. Just show me where the cells are.'

Slater reached for the keys and made his way towards the cells. He couldn't imagine what the caller was doing here at this ungodly hour, but he wasn't about to question him. 'They're this way, sir.'

Thomas had just finished filling his pipe when he had seen the rider approach the cabin where Anderson had told him Linford and Cropper where being held. This was the second night that he'd stood guard since he had been ordered to leave the garrison three days ago following Jameson's death, and he wasn't too pleased. He had already decided that if nothing happened by the time he'd finished smoking his freshly filled pipe, then he would head back to Rose Cropper's house. It had been Anderson's idea to stake out the building and Thomas intended telling him that he could take his turn for the next couple of nights.

Maybe someone with better sight might have identified the rider in uniform, but whoever it was shouldn't have been here at this time of night. If Thomas was a betting man his money would have been on it being Anderson, especially after General

Mosley's warning. Thomas was thinking that the jumpy soldier who was on guard might have wet his pants when his unexpected visitor arrived. He untied his saddled horse from the bushes behind him, having decided to ride the short distance to the cabin in case he had to give chase after whoever was interested in visiting the prisoners at this time of night. Thomas was also anxious to get to the cabin as quickly as possible, concerned that the soldier on guard might be in danger, and he urged his mount forward at speed. The bay hitched outside the cabin didn't look familiar to him, but that didn't mean that it wasn't Anderson inside. As Thomas was easing back the reins to slow his mount down, he saw a figure emerge from the doorway. He couldn't see the man's features, but he could see the raised arm that was in a firing position. The bullet that was intended for Thomas missed the target due to the man snatching at the shot, perhaps taken by the surprise of Thomas's arrival or because of the poor light. Thomas's return fire ripped into the man's chest causing him to cry out, before he pitched forward on to the ground at the bottom of the steps. Thomas was too experienced to take any chances and after he'd dismounted he kicked the man's pistol away, ensuring that it was out of reach.

Thomas climbed the porch steps anxious to discover the fate of the guard rather than check the identity of the man he had probably just killed. Thomas gave a despairing groan when saw that he was too late. Slater's throat had been cut, probably after he had been hit from behind, judging by the wound on the back of his head. At least he had been spared the gasp for air as the blood had spurted on to the floor. Thomas made his way to the cells expecting to see more carnage but could only say, 'Holy shit, what the hell's going on?' when he saw that the cells were empty.

He made his way back to the porch, curious to see who he had shot and wondering if the man was dead, but he was soon facing a gun for the second time. It was being held by another man in uniform. This time Thomas did recognize the horse which belonged to Captain Anderson.

Thomas braced himself. 'I don't know what all this is about, Anderson, but I guess General Mosley was right to warn me about you.'

Anderson smiled as he started to holster his gun. 'Then why did you shoot him, Marshal?'

Thomas looked towards the figure on the ground and in the clearer light from the opened door he saw the insignia on the uniform that belonged to a general. Thomas shook his head when he turned the body over and saw the staring eyes of General Mosley.

Thomas felt the anger rise in him. 'You knew that he would come here, didn't you? When you told me to tell him where Major Linford was, it was as bait for him, and not his adjutant. Why didn't you tell me? And why didn't you warn that soldier who's lying back there in his own blood?'

Anderson was about to explain to Thomas that he was under strict orders not to reveal the details of the plan, but he didn't get the chance. He should have stayed mounted while he gave his reason and was soon sprawled on the ground, stroking a badly split cheek.

'The whole thing stinks, Anderson, and I'm heading home right now before I do something that I'll regret.'

'I don't blame you for feeling as you do, but when we get back to the garrison, my CO will explain why it had to be done this way. It's all over now, but there are still some things you need to know.'

Thomas mounted his horse and rode off without speaking to Anderson, intending to pick up his things from the Cropper house before heading home to Statton Crossing.

FOURTEEN

Apart from Sheriff Luckings, none of the folks of Statton Crossing knew what had happened to Thomas, except that he had been sent to prison because of some big mistake. So he was able to settle into a life of retirement without feeling that folks were talking behind his back. He'd thought about Anderson from time to time and wondered if perhaps he'd been hard on him.

Thomas had enjoyed long days, and sometimes nights fishing, but he was restless and it hadn't gone unnoticed by Len Luckings who was not far off retiring himself. 'You miss the old job, don't you, Ned?' Luckings asked him, when they were sitting in the sheriff's office. 'How long have you been back?' he asked, before Thomas could answer the first question.

'I've been back exactly two months, Len, and I don't miss the old job. Not in the way that you think, but I just don't feel settled. Too many loose ends I guess.'

Luckings asked him what he meant and Thomas just replied, 'It's a long story, and too confusing to explain. Let's just say that I might have misjudged someone, and I'll probably end my days still wondering about certain things.'

Luckings watched Thomas leave, and felt sorry for him, knowing that his friend was only a shadow of the man who had always seemed in control of things.

Three days after Luckings had listened to a sad Thomas, he saw him heading towards the railway station.

'Well, you ain't going fishing, Ned,' Luckings said, 'and I know you don't go to church, so where are you heading for all spruced up? You look naked without a gun strapped to your middle.'

'I've been summoned to Dalham Garrison,' Thomas replied, sounding almost excited. 'According to the letter I received yesterday it will be to my advantage and all expenses will be paid. So I thought why not give the fish a rest. I should be back next week and then I'm off on my travels again, but I'll tell you about that when I get back.' Luckings smiled as he watched Thomas stride off with a new spring in his step.

The journey to Dalham was uneventful and he was disappointed to find that the train no longer stopped at Saratone Station, so he wouldn't be able to find out what happened to Tyler, the confidence trickster.

Upon his arrival in Dalham, he was met at the station by a young officer and directed to a waiting carriage which brought back memories of his meeting with Linford and the events that followed. He'd wondered what had happened to Linford and was hoping that it wasn't anything pleasant.

Thomas had expected to be taken to the garrison, but the carriage drew up outside the government building where he had his meetings with Stanmore. He was even taken to the same section of the building, and directed by the adjutant to Stanmore's old office. Thomas shook his head in bewilderment when he saw the name on the door and was once again wondering what the hell was going on.

'Good to see you again, Marshal, and thanks for coming. Sorry about the cryptic note. Please take a seat. There's a lot to talk about,' said Colonel Linford.

Thomas had never warmed to Linford even before he'd discovered that he was suspected of being involved in the kidnap. Seeing the smiling face of a man whom he'd hoped would be rotting in prison, or dead, left him more dumbfounded than ever.

'I expect seeing me here must be a bit bewildering, Marshal, but I promise that by the time you leave here everything will be clear to you. There'll be the odd bit of information that must remain classified, but there'll be no lies or cover ups. Now, let me pour you a drink. I expect you'll be needing it.'

Thomas was pleased when Linford filled the glass full to the brim with brandy and he would accept a few refills before the meeting was over.

'First of all, as you have probably realized, I was never involved in the kidnap, at least not in any criminal way.'

'Then why did Captain Anderson tell me that you were?' asked Thomas, remembering his conversation with Anderson.

'Captain Anderson was acting under orders when he told you that. It was all part of the plan, as was making you believe that Cropper was still alive, when he had already been killed by a jealous husband. But, of course, I was involved in the kidnap investigation. Colonel Clayton was in fact an alias of mine. Anderson was working for me.'

'I don't follow,' Thomas growled still not trusting him.

'I'm afraid you'll need to be patient and I can understand how it must appear to you. Let me try and clear up a few things first, although I might repeat some things that you have already been told by Anderson. It was me who passed the note to you, but it wasn't under General Stanmore's direction. You were told it was Stanmore to make it appear that I was up to no good and that I only helped you under Stanmore's orders.'

'So who killed the general?' Thomas asked.

'The general's admin officer, Captain Craddock, came forward after it became known that General Mosley was dead and told us that Mosley had visited

General Stanmore before you were supposed to have seen him. You might remember that when Craddock was questioned in court, he was only asked if anyone visited the general *after* you, not before. Craddock admitted that it was possible that he might have been busy when you passed him after you had decided not to call on the general. Craddock was pretty upset that he might have helped send you to prison and he has resigned from the service.'

'Mosley killed General Stanmore?' Thomas asked, before taking a gulp of brandy.

'We believe that he did. He must have got someone to steal your knife.'

'But why would he do it, and why did he end up murdering an innocent soldier who was guarding empty cells in a rundown farmhouse? It just doesn't make sense, and where did Captain Jameson fit into this?'

'Hmm, it's all a bit involved really. Mosley and Stanmore planned to get the lion's share of the ransom money. They were both approaching retirement and probably seized the opportunity to take over the kidnap for their own benefit. Captain Jameson was working for Mosley and we believe he planned to kill everyone who was at Old Dalham, including you, the Carters, Cropper and the private who accompanied him that day.'

Thomas questioned what he'd just been told. 'That doesn't explain why General Stanmore was killed, or why he was involved, because he was already a wealthy man!'

'Stanmore had frittered away his fortune on drink and gambling. His share of the ransom would have helped see out his days in the style he was accustomed to. We can't be absolutely certain why Mosley killed Stanmore, but it seems likely that he blamed him for the loss of the ransom money. It's also possible that Mosley did it to prevent Stanmore from letting something out during one of his drunken ramblings.'

Thomas was relieved that he hadn't misjudged Stanmore after all, but he was puzzled why Stanmore was so pleased after the kidnap operation, if his retirement plans had just been ruined. He addressed his concerns about Stanmore's reaction with Linford.

'I was puzzled as well and expected him to be gunning for whoever had warned you about the tampered gun, but he didn't even question me about it, even though I would have been a suspect. I can only assume that he was looking forward to being praised for a successful operation. Ironically the success of the operation may have eased his financial worries because he might have been given a plum civilian job, but Mosley wouldn't have bene-fited in the same way.'

'So why was Mosley so concerned about you being arrested?' Thomas asked, still not certain how it all fitted as neatly as Linford was claiming.

'He probably thought that I might have known what Stanmore was up to, but wasn't bothered until I was supposedly arrested, and the case reopened. When you came back on the scene he probably feared that something might be uncovered. Like so many parts of this case we can only speculate. Mosley certainly didn't know that I was working for special operations.'

Thomas was still thinking it was all far fetched when he said, 'So that's what the "flushing out" was all about.'

'That was Anderson's idea, but we have you to thank for the success of that. It seems likely that Mosley ordered Captain Jameson to kill you, perhaps intending it as a warning to Anderson to back off, or perhaps they both wanted revenge against you. With Jameson dead, the general had no one he could trust to do his dirty work. I guess he panicked and that's why he tried to come after me and Cropper, fearing that we were a threat to him. The truth is that the investigation had produced no real evidence against him, and if he had just kept his nerve he would have been safe from being exposed.'

'Is it true about Cropper being dead?' Thomas asked, thinking once more about Rose Cropper.

'I'm afraid so. That was another lie that I asked Anderson to tell you.'

Thomas sighed. 'I think I might owe young Anderson an apology, and I can finally thank you for the warning note. Well, I was hoping that some of the loose ends would get tidied up one day, but I never figured anything like you've just told me. Does all this mean that I'll be declared innocent?'

Linford looked at the clock on the wall opposite

before he replied. 'You'll have to wait a little longer before the final chapter is told, but I expect you'll want to see Captain Anderson first.' Linford smiled before he added, 'You might want to drink some strong coffee while you are with him.'

Thomas was feeling much better after he had spoken to Anderson in his office in the same building. They were joking about the punch he had floored Anderson with when they were outside the farmhouse just after Mosley's death, when Linford appeared and declared, 'Time for us to go, gentlemen.'

'What's all this about. Not more surprises?' Thomas queried.

'All in good time, Marshal,' replied Linford, but Thomas didn't see him wink at Anderson.

When the three men entered the hall, the gathering of civilians and military personnel stood and applauded. Thomas intended to have words with Anderson when this was over, but it would only be words this time.

The trio were directed to seats on the raised platform, but were soon standing up when the Vice President was introduced. He opened his speech by explaining that the President regretted that the ceremony was not being held in Washington in his presence and that the awards could not be given the publicity they deserved. Linford and Anderson were the first to receive their special awards for their outstanding investigative work. When the applause had died down, the colonel conducting the presentation announced, 'The two final awards go to Marshal Ned Thomas. The first is the highest military award for bravery, and the second is the highest award that a President can bestow on a civilian. A full explanation as to how these awards were earned can never been revealed for security reasons, but suffice it to say that they are truly deserving because of the recipient's dedication, bravery and personal sacrifice.'

Thomas was a modest man, but he was proud of the personal recognition that meant much more to him than any publicity would have done. He was pleased for Anderson and Linford, and it meant that he could retire with satisfaction now that the record had been put straight.

He was still getting over the surprise of what had happened when the Vice President stood up again.

'I do have one final award for Marshal Thomas if he would please step forward.'

When Anderson saw the look on Thomas's face after the US Marshal's badge had been pinned to his chest he had little doubt which award meant most to him.

After the ceremony was over, Anderson escorted Thomas out of the building to a waiting carriage that would take Thomas to his hotel where he would spend the night before catching the train home in the morning. He was about to step into the carriage when he turned in the direction of the neighing sound behind him and saw a black stallion being led by a soldier.

Thomas turned to a smiling Anderson and said,

'What a beauty. He's identical to my old horse except for the white flash on his nose being a bit wider.'

'I promise you that this is the last surprise of the day. He's yours, Marshal. He's a gift from the army. I'm afraid he's not as well bred as your old horse, but as you say, he's a beauty.'

The events of the day finally got to him and he needed to swallow hard before he thanked Anderson.

Two days later, Anderson was at the station to help board the stallion and say his farewell.

'I expect you'll be looking forward to being back on duty,' Anderson said. 'But at least you won't have to worry about doing all the paperwork and sitting behind a desk. The plan is for you to double up with your old friend, Marshal Patterson. He'll do the administration, and you can pick and choose what you want to do. I expect you'll just want to phase your work towards your retirement in easy steps.'

Thomas was pleased to hear about his future role because he hadn't been relishing the idea of sitting behind a desk or giving orders to his deputies. He had already been told that the financial arrangements for his new position had been sorted out, and he didn't plan to work for very long.

'That's a relief; I wasn't looking forward to pushing a pen, but it'll be good to start work again after I've made a special trip first. It was something that I promised myself I would do. It won't take long, perhaps a week.'

Anderson was curious and said, 'It sounds interesting. Why is it so special?'

'I'm going to visit the Yukron Valley Prison and see a few old friends; well, they ain't exactly friends, but I would like to see them. If I don't go now, I probably never will, and I'd feel bad about that.'

Thomas figured that Motton's body would have been picked clean a long time ago, and if it was ever found it would be unrecognizable, but there was always a chance that it might have been recovered. He asked Anderson if Motton had ever been tracked down, but he really wanted to know if his body had been found.

'I wouldn't know,' replied Anderson, 'but, I believe that Johnson took over as head guard, and I hope things have improved since my visit. Will you be sending them a wire to let them know you're planning to visit?'

Thomas was thoughtful for a moment. 'I suppose I should, but I was thinking of just riding up to the main gate. I suppose it'll be a bit of a surprise for Johnson and the rest of the guards. I had better make sure that they can see my shiny new marshal's badge. Mind you, if the prisoners really did believe that I'm buried close by, then I hope they'll see the funny side of it. I daresay Johnson and the guards will have thought that my bones are rotting somewhere in the desert.'

Thomas laughed at the thought, without realizing just how much of a shock his reappearance

would be to Clay Johnson who might never know
who it was that he had mistakenly shot that day,
thinking it was Thomas. In the same way that
Thomas might never know that Motton wasn't dead
when he'd left him against the rocks as he rode off
on Motton's horse.